E8

P9

6—

Bible Stories for
ADULTS

❖

Also by James Morrow

Towing Jehovah

City of Truth

Nebula Awards 26, 27, *and* 28 *(editor)*

Only Begotten Daughter

This Is the Way the World Ends

The Continent of Lies

The Wine of Violence

Bible Stories for
ADULTS

❖

JAMES MORROW

A Harvest Original
Harcourt Brace & Company
SAN DIEGO   NEW YORK   LONDON

Copyright © 1996, 1994, 1992, 1991, 1990, 1989, 1988, 1987, 1984
by James Morrow

All rights reserved. No part of this publication
may be reproduced or transmitted in any form or by any means,
electronic or mechanical, including photocopy, recording,
or any information storage and retrieval system,
without permission in writing from the publisher.

Requests for permission to make copies
of any part of the work should be mailed to:
Permissions Department, Harcourt Brace & Company,
6277 Sea Harbor Drive, Orlando, Florida 32887-6777.

Library of Congress Cataloging-in-Publication Data
Morrow, James, 1947–
   Bible stories for adults/James Morrow.
      p.   cm.
   ISBN 0-15-100192-8.—ISBN 0-15-600244-2 (pbk: A Harvest original)
   1. Science fiction, American. 2. Satire, American. I. Title.
PS3563.0876B5   1996
813'.54—dc20   95-36805

Text set in Sabon
Designed by Judythe Sieck

Printed in the United States of America
GFEDCB

Publication acknowledgments appear on page 245,
which constitutes a continuation of the copyright page.

CONTENTS

PREFACE

There are two kinds of people in the world, those who believe the Bible is an anthology and those who believe it is a collection. Do the Scriptures trace to many minds, or were they dictated by a single Author? As the year 2001 approaches, this controversy will grow increasingly acute. The Parousia may get postponed, Jesus may neglect to come, Judgment Day may decline to dawn, but the one thing we *do* know the turn of the millennium will bring is millennialism. It will bring prophecies, predictions, and plays for power by those for whom the Bible is the "Word of God." People who prefer the anthology theory of Bible origins, meanwhile, may experience a strong impulse to head for the hills. Myself, I intend to roll up my sleeves, fire up my computer, and continue rewriting Holy Writ as subversively as I can.

Four of the stories in the present collection are overt critiques of famous Bible tales: a deconstruction of the Flood legend, a follow-up to the Tower of Babel fable, an alternative climax to Moses' theophany on Sinai, and the further fulminations of Job. The Judeo-Christian worldview also informs "Daughter Earth," with its unprecedented nativity; "Spelling God with the Wrong Blocks," my attempt to stand so-called creation science on its head; and "Diary of a Mad Deity," which purports to explain why Yahweh possesses the authoritarian personality he so frequently exhibits in the Torah.

Monotheism is just one of the myths by which we live, and Yahweh is just one of the deities who populate these stories. Powering the plot of "Known But to God and Wilbur Hines" is the dark god of nationalism. "The Confessions of Ebenezer Scrooge" exploits Dickens's morality tale to ask whether charity alone can exorcise the demons that drive monopoly capitalism. "Arms and the Woman" considers the *Iliad* as a tract celebrating the cult of organized warfare.

Eschatological themes are not the only ones that fascinate me. "The Assemblage of Kristin" uses ghost-story conventions to address the mystery of consciousness; "Abe Lincoln in McDonald's" considers the notion that middle-class America would have far less difficulty accommodating chattel slavery than is commonly supposed; motifs of procreation, parenting, feminism, and epistemology figure throughout these pages. Nevertheless, religion remains the obsession I am most often called upon to defend. Whenever one of my send-ups of the sacred appears in a magazine, I can expect a letter from a churchgoer informing me that I missed the point of whichever scriptural passages I was trying to flay. Meanwhile, my friends in the nouveau paganism camp accuse me of quaintness: Bible thumpers are straw men, so why bother? (In this view, my efforts amount to what P. J. O'Rourke calls "hunting dairy cows with a high-powered rifle and scope.") My answer is that straw men, once set aflame with zeal, can be quite dangerous and that the gap between New Age irrationalism and Christian fundamentalism is not nearly so wide as we might wish to believe.

Much to my delight, Harcourt Brace has elected to release *Bible Stories for Adults* in tandem with a trade paperback reprint of my 1990 novel, *Only Begotten Daughter*, an inquiry into a neglected branch of Jesus' family tree. Together, these two volumes can be taken as a science-fiction satirist's responses to the Old Testament and the New Testament respectively. While the meanings of the present stories and *Only Begotten Daughter* may be ambiguous, their source—as far as I can tell—is not. To the best of my knowledge, all issue from the same bewildered pilgrim operating with a single befuddled brain.

James Morrow
State College, Pennsylvania
September 11, 1995

Bible Stories for Adults, No. 17: The Deluge

❖

TAKE YOUR CUP down to the Caspian, dip, and drink. It did not always taste of salt. Yahweh's watery slaughter may have purified the earth, but it left his seas a ruin, brackish with pagan blood and the tears of wicked orphans.

Sheila and her generation know the deluge is coming. Yahweh speaks to them through their sins. A thief cuts a purse, and the shekels clank together, pealing out a call to repentance. A priest kneels before a graven image of Dagon, and the statue opens its marble jaws, issuing not its own warnings but Yahweh's. A harlot threads herself with a thorny vine, tearing out unwanted flesh, and a divine voice rises from the bleeding fetus. You are a corrupt race, Yahweh says, abominable in my sight. My rains will scrub you from the earth.

Yahweh is as good as his word. The storm breaks. Creeks become rivers, rivers cataracts. Lakes blossom into broiling, wrathful seas.

Yes, Sheila is thoroughly foul in those days, her apple home to many worms, the scroll of her sins as long as the Araxas. She is gluttonous and unkempt. She sells her body. Her abortions number eleven. *I should have made it twelve,* she realizes on the day the deluge begins. But it is too late, she had already gone through with it—the labor more agonizing than any abortion, her breasts left pulpy and deformed—and soon the boy was seven, athletic, clever, fair of face, but today the swift feet are clamped in the cleft of an olive-tree root, the clever hands are still, the fair face lies buried in water.

A mother, Sheila has heard, should be a boat to her child, buoying him up during floods, bearing him through storms, and yet it is Sam who rescues her. She is hoisting his corpse aloft, hoping to drain the death from his lungs, when suddenly his little canoe floats by. A scooped-out log, nothing more, but still his favorite toy. He liked to paddle it across the Araxas and catch turtles in the marsh.

Sheila climbs aboard, leaving Sam's meat to the sharks.

Captain's Log. 10 June 1057 After Creation

The beasts eat too much. At present rates of consumption, we'll be out of provisions in a mere fifteen weeks.

For the herbivores: 4,540 pounds of oats a day, 6,780 pounds of hay, 2,460 of vegetables, and 3,250 of fruit.

For the carnivores: 17,620 pounds of yak and caribou meat a day. And we may lose the whole supply if we don't find a way to freeze it.

Yahweh's displeasure pours down in great swirling sheets, as if the planet lies fixed beneath a waterfall. Sheila paddles without passion, no goal in mind, no reason to live. Fierce winds churn the sea. Lightning shatters the sky. The floodwaters thicken with disintegrating sinners, afloat on their backs, their gelatinous eyes locked in pleading stares, as if begging God for a second chance.

The world reeks. Sheila gags on the vapors. Is the decay of the wicked, she wonders, more odoriferous than that of the just? When she dies, will her stink drive away even flies and vultures?

Sheila wants to die, but her flesh argues otherwise, making her lift her mouth toward heaven and swallow the quenching downpour. The hunger will be harder to solve: it hurts, a scorpion stinging her belly, so painful that Sheila resolves to add cannibalism to her repertoire. But then, in the bottom of the canoe, she spies two huddled turtles, confused, fearful. She eats one raw, beginning with the head, chewing the leathery tissues, drinking the salty blood.

A dark, mountainous shape cruises out of the blur. A sea monster, she decides, angry, sharp-toothed, ravenous . . . Yahweh incarnate, eager to rid the earth of Sheila. Fine. Good. Amen. Painfully she lifts her paddle, heavy as a millstone, and strokes through a congestion of drowned princes and waterlogged horses, straight for the hulking deity.

Now God is upon her, a headlong collision, fracturing the canoe like a crocodile's tail smacking an egg. The floodwaters cover her, a frigid darkness flows through her, and with her last breath she lobs a sphere of mucus into Yahweh's gloomy and featureless face.

CAPTAIN'S LOG. 20 JUNE 1057 A.C.

Yahweh said nothing about survivors. Yet this morning we came upon two.

The Testudo marginata *posed no problem. We have plenty of turtles, all two hundred and twenty-five species in fact, Testudinidae, Chelydridae, Platysternidae, Kinosternidae, Chelonidae, you name it. Unclean beasts, inedible, useless. We left it to the flood. Soon it will swim itself to death.*

The Homo sapiens *was a different matter. Frightened, delirious, she clung to her broken canoe like a sloth embracing a tree. "Yahweh was explicit," said Ham, leaning over* Eden II's *rail, calling into the gushing storm. "Every person not in this family deserves death."*

"She is one of the tainted generation," added his wife. "A whore. Abandon her."

"No," countered Japheth. "We must throw her a line, as any men of virtue would do."

His young bride had no opinion.

As for Shem and Tamar, the harlot's arrival became yet another occasion for them to bicker. "Japheth is right," insisted Shem. "Bring her among us, Father."

"Let Yahweh have his way with her," retorted Tamar. "Let the flood fulfill its purpose."

"What do you think?" I asked Reumah.

Smiling softly, my wife pointed to the dinghy.

I ordered the little boat lowered. Japheth and Shem rode it to the surface of the lurching sea, prying the harlot from her canoe, hauling her over the transom. After much struggle we got her aboard Eden II, laying her unconscious bulk on the foredeck. She was a lewd walrus, fat and dissipated. A chain of rat skulls dangled from her squat neck. When Japheth pushed on her chest, water fountained out, and she released a cough like a yak's roar.

"Who are you?" I demanded.

She fixed me with a dazed stare and fainted. We carried her below, setting her among the pigs like the unclean thing she is. Reumah stripped away our visitor's soggy garments, and I winced to behold her pocked and twisted flesh.

"Sinner or not, Yahweh has seen fit to spare her,"
said my wife, wrapping a dry robe around the
harlot. "We are the instruments of his amnesty."

"Perhaps," I said, snapping the word like a whip.

The final decision rests with me, of course, not
with my sons or their wives. Is the harlot a test?
Would a true God-follower sink this human flot-
sam without a moment's hesitation?

Even asleep, our visitor is vile, her hair a lice
farm, her breath a polluting wind.

Sheila awakens to the snorty gossip of pigs. A great bowl
of darkness envelops her, dank and dripping like a basket
submerged in a swamp. Her nostrils burn with a hundred
varieties of stench. She believes that Yahweh has swallowed her, that she is imprisoned in his maw.

Slowly a light seeps into her eyes. Before her, a wooden
gate creaks as it pivots on leather hinges. A young man
approaches, proffering a wineskin and a cooked leg of
mutton.

"Are we inside God?" Sheila demands, propping her
thick torso on her elbows. Someone has given her dry
clothes. The effort of speaking tires her, and she lies back
in the swine-scented straw. "Is this Yahweh?"

"The last of his creation," the young man replies.
"My parents, brothers, our wives, the birds, beasts—and
myself, Japheth. Here. Eat." Japheth presses the mutton
to her lips. "Seven of each clean animal, that was our

quota. In a month we shall run out. Enjoy it while you can."

"I want to die." Once again, Sheila's abundant flesh has a different idea, devouring the mutton, guzzling the wine.

"If you wanted to die," says Japheth, "you would not have gripped that canoe so tightly. Welcome aboard."

"Aboard?" says Sheila. Japheth is most handsome. His crisp black beard excites her lust. "We're on a boat?"

Japheth nods. "*Eden II.* Gopher wood, stem to stern. This is the world now, nothing else remains. Yahweh means for you to be here."

"I doubt that." Sheila knows her arrival is a freak. She has merely been overlooked. No one means for her to be here, least of all God.

"My father built it," the young man explains. "He is six hundred years old."

"Impressive," says Sheila, grimacing. She has seen the type, a crotchety, withered patriarch, tripping over his beard. Those final five hundred years do nothing for a man, save to make his skin leathery and his worm boneless.

"You're a whore, aren't you?" asks Japheth.

The boat pitches and rolls, unmooring Sheila's stomach. She lifts the wineskin to her lips and fills her pouchy cheeks. "Also a drunkard, thief, self-abortionist"—her grin stretches well into the toothless regions—"and sexual deviant." With her palm she cradles her left breast, heaving it to one side.

Japheth gasps and backs away.

Another day, perhaps, they will lie together. For now, Sheila is exhausted, stunned by wine. She rests her reeling head on the straw and sleeps.

Captain's Log. 25 June 1057 A.C.

We have harvested a glacier, bringing thirty tons of ice aboard. For the moment, our meat will not become carrion; our tigers, wolves, and carnosaurs will thrive.

I once saw the idolators deal with an outcast. They tethered his ankles to an ox, his wrists to another ox. They drove the first beast north, the second south.

Half of me believes we must admit this woman. Indeed, if we kill her, do we not become the same people Yahweh saw fit to destroy? If we so sin, do we not contaminate the very race we are meant to sire? In my sons' loins rests the whole of the future. We are the keepers of our kind. Yahweh picked us for the purity of our seed, not the infallibility of our justice. It is hardly our place to condemn.

My other half begs that I cast her into the flood. A harlot, Japheth assures me. A dipsomaniac, robber, lesbian, and fetus-killer. She should have died with the rest of them. We must not allow her degenerate womb back into the world, lest it bear fruit.

Again Sheila awakens to swine sounds, refreshed and at peace. She no longer wishes to die.

This afternoon a different brother enters the pig cage. He gives his name as Shem, and he is even better looking than Japheth. He bears a glass of tea in which float three diaphanous pebbles. "Ice," he explains. "Clotted water."

Sheila drinks. The frigid tea buffs the grime from her tongue and throat. Ice: a remarkable material, she decides. These people know how to live.

"Do you have a piss pot?" Sheila asks, and Shem guides her to a tiny stall enclosed by reed walls. After she has relieved herself, Shem gives her a tour, leading her up and down the ladders that connect the interior decks. *Eden II* leaks like a defective tent, a steady, disquieting plop-plop.

The place is a zoo. Mammals, reptiles, birds, two by two. Sheila beholds tiny black beasts with too many legs and long cylindrical creatures with too few. Grunts, growls, howls, roars, brays, and caws rattle the ship's wet timbers.

Sheila likes Shem, but not this floating menagerie, this crazy voyage. The whole arrangement infuriates her. Cobras live here. Wasps, their stingers poised to spew poisons. Young tyrannosaurs and baby allosaurs, eager to devour the gazelles on the deck above. Tarantulas, rats, crabs, weasels, armadillos, snapping turtles, boar-pigs, bacteria, viruses: Yahweh has spared them all.

My friends were no worse than a tarantula, Sheila thinks. My neighbors were as important as weasels. My child mattered more than anthrax.

Captain's Log. 14 July 1057 A.C.

The rains have stopped. We drift aimlessly. Reumah is seasick. Even with the ice, our provisions are running out. We cannot keep feeding ourselves, much less a million species.

Tonight we discussed our passenger. Predictably, Japheth and Shem spoke for acquittal, while Ham argued the whore must die.

"A necessary evil?" I asked Ham.

"No kind of evil," he replied. "You kill a rabid dog lest its disease spread, Father. This woman's body holds the eggs of future thieves, perverts, and idolators. We must not allow her to infect the new order. We must check this plague before our chance is lost."

"We have no right," said Japheth.

"If God can pass a harsh judgment on millions of evildoers," said Ham, "then surely I can do the same for one."

"You are not God," said Japheth.

Nor am I—but I am the master of this ship, the leader of this little tribe. I turned to Ham and said, "I know you speak the truth. We must choose ultimate good over immediate mercy."

Ham agreed to be her executioner. Soon he will dispose of the whore using the same obsidian knife with which, once we sight land, we are

bound to slit and drain our surplus lambs, grati-
tude's blood.

They have put Sheila to work. She and Ham must maintain the reptiles. The Pythoninae will not eat unless they kill the meal themselves. Sheila spends the whole afternoon competing with the cats, snaring ship rats, hurling them by their tails into the python pens.

Ham is the handsomest son yet, but Sheila does not care for him. There is something low and slithery about Ham. It seems fitting that he tends vipers and asps.

"What do you think of Yahweh?" she asks.

Instead of answering, Ham leers.

"When a father is abusive," Sheila persists, "the child typically responds not only by denying that the abuse occurred, but by redoubling his efforts to be loved."

Silence from Ham. He fondles her with his eyes.

Sheila will not quit. "When I destroyed my unwanted children, it was murder. When Yahweh did the same, it was eugenics. Do you approve of the universe, Ham?"

Ham tosses the python's mate a rat.

CAPTAIN'S LOG. 17 JULY 1057 A.C.

We have run aground. Shem has named the place
of our imprisonment Ararat. This morning we
sent out a Corvus corax, *but it did not return. I*
doubt we'll ever see it again. Two ravens remain,
but I refuse to break up a pair. Next time we'll
try a Columbidae.

In an hour the harlot will die. Ham will open her up, spilling her dirty blood, her filthy organs. Together we shall cast her carcass into the flood.

Why did Yahweh say nothing about survivors?

Silently Ham slithers into the pig cage, crouching over Sheila like an incubus, resting the cool blade against her windpipe.

Sheila is ready. Japheth has told her the whole plot. A sudden move, and Ham's universe is awry, Sheila above, her attacker below, she armed, he defenseless. She wriggles her layered flesh, pressing Ham into the straw. Her scraggly hair tickles his cheeks.

A rape is required. Sheila is good at rape; some of her best customers would settle for nothing less. Deftly she steers the knife amid Ham's garments, unstitching them, peeling him like an orange. "Harden," she commands, fondling his pods, running a practiced hand across his worm. "Harden or die."

Ham shudders and sweats. Terror flutes his lips, but before he can cry out Sheila slides the knife across his throat like a bow across a fiddle, delicately dividing the skin, drawing out tiny beads of blood.

Sheila is a professional. She can stiffen eunuchs, homosexuals, men with knives at their jugulars. Lifting her robe, she lowers herself onto Ham's erection, enjoying his pleasureless passion, reveling in her impalement. A few minutes of graceful undulation, and the worm spurts, filling her with Ham's perfect and upright seed.

"I want to see your brothers," she tells him.

"What?" Ham touches his throat, reopening his fine, subtle wound.

"Shem and Japheth also have their parts to play."

CAPTAIN'S LOG. 24 JULY 1057 A.C.

Our dinghy is missing. Maybe the whore cut it loose before she was executed. No matter. This morning I launched a dove, and it has returned with a twig of some kind in its beak. Soon our sandals will touch dry land.

My sons elected to spare me the sight of the whore's corpse. Fine. I have beheld enough dead sinners in my six centuries.

Tonight we shall sing, dance, and give thanks to Yahweh. Tonight we shall bleed our best lamb.

The world is healing. Cool, smooth winds rouse Sheila's hair, sunlight strokes her face. Straight ahead, white robust clouds sail across a clear sky.

A speck hovers in the distance, and Sheila fixes on it as she navigates the boundless flood. This sign has appeared none too soon. The stores from *Eden II* will not last through the week, especially with Sheila's appetite at such a pitch.

Five weeks in the dinghy, and still her period has not come. "And Ham's child is just the beginning," she mutters, tossing a wry smile toward the clay pot. So far, the ice shows no sign of melting; Shem and Japheth's virtuous fertilizer, siphoned under goad of lust and threat of death, remains frozen. Sheila has plundered enough seed to fill all creation with babies. If things go according to plan, Yahweh will have to stage another flood.

The speck grows, resolves into a bird. A *Corvus corax,* as the old man would have called it.

Sheila will admit that her designs are grand and even pompous. But are they impossible? She aims to found a proud and impertinent nation, a people driven to decipher ice and solve the sun, each of them with as little use for obedience as she, and they will sail the sodden world until they find the perfect continent, a land of eternal light and silken grass, and they will call it what any race must call its home, Formosa, beautiful.

The raven swoops down, landing atop the jar of sperm, and Sheila feels a surge of gladness as, reaching out, she takes a branch from its sharp and tawny beak.

Daughter Earth

❖

WE'D BEEN TRYING to have another child for over three
years, carrying on like a couple from one of those movies
you can rent by going behind the beaded curtain at Jake's
Video, but it just wasn't working out. Logic, of course,
says a second conception should prove no harder than a
first. Hah. Mother Nature can be a sneaky old bitch,
something we've learned from our twenty-odd years of
farming down here in central Pennsylvania.

Maybe you've driven past our place, Garber Farm,
two miles outside of Boalsburg on Route 322. Raspberries in the summer, apples in the fall, Christmas trees in
the winter, asparagus in the spring—that's us. The basset
hound puppies appear all year round. We'll sell you one
for three hundred dollars, guaranteed to love the children, chase rabbits out of the vegetable patch, and always appear burdened by troubles greater than yours.

We started feeling better after Dr. Borealis claimed he could make Polly's uterus "more hospitable to reproduction," as he put it. He prescribed vaginal suppositories, little nuggets of progesterone packed in cocoa butter. You store them in the refrigerator till you're ready to use one, and they melt in your wife the way M&Ms melt in your mouth.

That very month, we got pregnant.

So there we were, walking around with clouds under our feet. We kept remembering our son's first year out of the womb, that sense of power we'd felt, how we'd just gone ahead and thought him up and made him, by damn.

Time came for the amniocentesis. It began with the ultrasound technician hooking Polly up to the TV monitor so Dr. Borealis could keep his syringe on target and make sure it didn't skewer the fetus. I liked Borealis. He reminded me of Norman Rockwell's painting of that tubby and fastidious old country doctor listening to the little girl's doll with his stethoscope.

Polly and I were hoping for a girl.

Oddly enough, the fetus wouldn't come into focus. Or, if it *was* in focus, it sure as hell didn't look like a fetus. I was awfully glad Polly couldn't see the TV.

"Glitch in the circuitry?" ventured the ultrasound technician, a tense and humorless youngster named Leo.

"Don't think so," muttered Borealis.

I used to be a center for my college basketball team,

the Penn State Nittany Lions, and I'll be damned if our baby didn't look a great deal like a basketball.

Possibly a soccer ball.

Polly said, "How is she?"

"Kind of round," I replied.

"Round, Ben? What do you mean?"

"Round," I said.

Borealis furrowed his brow, real deep ridges; you could've planted corn up there. "Now don't fret, Polly. You neither, Ben. If it's a tumor, it's probably benign."

"Round?" Polly said again.

"Round," I said again.

"Let's go for the juice anyway," the doctor told Leo the technician. "Maybe the lab can interpret this for us."

So Borealis gave Polly a local and then inserted his syringe, and suddenly the TV showed the needle poking around next to our fetus like a dipstick somebody was trying to get back into a Chevy. The doctor went ahead as if he were doing a normal amnio, gently pricking the sac, though I could tell he hadn't made peace with the situation, and I was feeling pretty miserable myself.

"Round?" said Polly.

"Right," I said.

Later that month, I was standing in the apple orchard harvesting some Jonafrees—a former basketball center doesn't need a ladder—when Asa, our eleven-year-old redheaded Viking, ran over and told me Borealis was on the phone. "Mom's napping," my son explained. "Being knocked up sure makes you tired, huh?"

I got to the kitchen as fast as I could. I snapped up the receiver, my questions spilling out helter-skelter— would Polly be okay, what kind of pregnancy was this, were they planning to set things right with *in utero* surgery?

Borealis said, "First of all, Polly's CA-125 reading is only nine, so it's probably not a malignancy."

"Thank God."

"And the fetus's chromosome count is normal— forty-six on the money. The surprising thing is that she has chromosomes at all."

"She? It's a *she?*"

"We'd like to do some more ultrasounds."

"It's a a *she?*"

"You bet, Ben. Two X chromosomes."

"Zenobia."

"Huh?"

"If we got a girl, we were going to name her Zenobia."

So we went back down to Boalsburg Gynecological. Borealis had called in three of his friends from the university: Gordon Hashigan, a spry old coot who held the Raymond Dart Chair in Physical Anthropology; Susan Croft, a stern-faced geneticist with a lisp; and Abner Logos, a skinny, devil-bearded epidemiologist who somehow found time to be Centre County's public health commissioner. Polly and I remembered voting against him.

Leo the technician connected Polly to his machine, snapping more pictures than a Japanese extended family takes when it visits Epcot Center, and then the three professors huddled solemnly around the printouts, mumbling to each other through thin, tight lips. Ten minutes later, they called Borealis over.

The doctor rolled up the printouts, tucked them under his arm, and escorted Polly and me into his office—a nicer, better-smelling office than the one we'd set up in the basset barn back home. He seemed nervous and apologetic. Sweat covered his temples like dew on a toadstool.

Borealis unfurled an ultrasound, and we saw how totally different our baby was from other babies. It wasn't just her undeniable sphericity—no, the real surprise was her complexion.

"It's like one of those Earth shots the astronauts send back when they're heading toward the moon," Polly noted.

Borealis nodded. "Here we've got a kind of ocean, for example. And this thing is like a continent."

"What's this?" I asked, pointing to a white mass near the bottom.

"Ice cap on the southern pole," said Borealis. "We can do the procedure next Tuesday."

"Procedure?" said Polly.

The doctor appeared to be experiencing a nasty odor.

"Polly, Ben, the simple fact is that I can't encourage you to bring this pregnancy to term. Those professors in the next room all agree."

My stomach churned sour milk.

"I thought the amnio was normal," said Polly.

"Try to understand," said Borealis. "This fetal tissue cannot be accurately labeled a baby."

"So what *do* you call it?" Polly demanded.

The doctor grimaced. "For the moment . . . a biosphere."

"A what?"

"Biosphere."

When Polly gets angry, she starts inflating—like a beach toy, or a puff adder, or a randy tree frog. "You're saying we can't give her a good home, is that it? Our *other* kid's turning out just fine. His project took second prize in the Centre County Science Fair."

"Organic Control of Gypsy Moths," I explained.

Borealis issued one of his elaborate frowns. "You really imagine yourself giving birth to this material?"

"Uh-huh," said Polly.

"But it's a biosphere."

"So what?"

The doctor squinched his cherubic Norman Rockwell face. "There's no way it's going to fit through the canal," he snapped, as if that settled the matter.

"So we're looking at a cesarean, huh?" said Polly.

Borealis threw up his hands as if he were dealing with a couple of dumb crackers. People think that being a

farmer means you're some sort of rube, though I've probably rented a lot more Ingmar Bergman videos than
Borealis—with subtitles, not dubbed—and the news-
letter we publish, *Down to Earth,* is a damned sight more
literate than those Pregnancy Pointers brochures the doctor kept shoveling at us. "Here's my home number," he
said, scribbling on his presciption pad. "Call me the minute anything happens."

The days slogged by. Polly kept swelling up with Zenobia, bigger and bigger, rounder and rounder, and by December she was so big and round she couldn't do
anything except crank out the Christmas issue of *Down
to Earth* on our Macintosh SE and waddle around the
farm like the *Hindenburg* looking for New Jersey. And
of course we couldn't have the expectant couple's usual
fun of imagining a new baby in the house. Every time I
stumbled into Zenobia's room and saw the crib and the
changing table and the Cookie Monster's picture on the
wall, my throat got tight as a stone. We cried a lot, Polly
and me. We'd crawl into bed and hug each other and
cry.

So it came as something of a relief when, one frosty
March morning, the labor pains started. Borealis
sounded pretty woozy when he answered the phone—it
was 3 A.M.—but he woke up fast, evidently pleased at
the idea of getting this biosphere business over with. I
think he was counting on a stillbirth.

"The contractions—how far apart?"

"Five minutes," I said.

"Goodness, that close? The thing's really on its way."

"We don't refer to her as a thing," I corrected him, politely but firmly.

By the time we got Asa over to my parents' house, the contractions were coming only four minutes apart. Polly started her Lamaze breathing. Except for its being a cesarean this time, and a biosphere, everything happened just like when we'd had our boy: racing down to Boalsburg Memorial; standing around in the lobby while Polly panted like a hot collie and the computer checked into our insurance; riding the elevator up to the maternity ward with Polly in a wheelchair and me fidgeting at her side; getting into our hospital duds—white gown for Polly, green surgical smock and cap for me. So far, so good.

Borealis was already in the OR. He'd brought along a mere skeleton crew. The assistant surgeon had a crisp, hawkish face organized around a nose so narrow you could've opened your mail with it. The anesthesiologist had the kind of tanned, handsome, Mediterranean features you see on condom boxes. The pediatric nurse was a gangly, owl-eyed young woman with freckles and pigtails. "I told them we're anticipating an anomaly," Borealis said, nodding toward his team.

"We don't call her an anomaly," I informed the doctor.

They positioned me by Polly's head—she was awake, anesthetized from the diaphragm down—right behind the white curtain they use to keep cesarean mothers from seeing too much. Borealis and his sidekick got to work. Basically, it was like watching a reverse-motion movie of somebody stuffing a turkey; the doctor made his incision and started rummaging around, and a few minutes later he scooped out an object that looked like a Rand McNally globe covered with vanilla frosting and olive oil.

"She's *here*," I shouted to Polly. Even though Zenobia wasn't a regular child, some sort of fatherly instinct kicked in, and my skin went prickly all over. "Our baby's *here*," I gasped, tears rolling down my cheeks.

"Holy mackerel!" said the assistant surgeon.

"Jesus!" said the anesthesiologist. "Jesus Lord God in heaven!"

"What the fuck?" said the pediatric nurse. "She's a fucking *ball*."

"Biosphere," Borealis admonished.

A loud, squishy, squalling noise filled the room: our little Zenobia, howling just like any other baby. "Is that her?" Polly wanted to know. "Is that *her* crying?"

"You bet it is, honey," I said.

Borealis handed Zenobia to the nurse and said, "Clean her up, Pam. Weigh her. All the usual."

The nurse said, "You've got to be fucking kidding."

"Clean her up," the doctor insisted.

Pam grabbed a sponge, dipped it into Zenobia's largest ocean, and began swabbing her northern hemisphere. Our child cooed and gurgled—and kept on cooing and gurgling as the nurse carried her across the room and set her on the scales.

"Nine pounds, six ounces," Pam announced.

"Ah, a *big* one," said Borealis, voice cracking. Zenobia, I could tell, had touched something deep inside him. His eyes were moist; the surgical lights twinkled in his tears. "Did you hear what a strong voice she has?" Now he worked on the placenta, carefully retrieving the soggy purple blob—it resembled a prop from one of those movies about zombie cannibals Asa was always renting from Jake's Video—all the while studying it carefully, as if it might contain some clue to Zenobia's peculiar anatomy. "You got her circumference yet?" he called.

The nurse gave him an oh-brother look and ran her tape measure around our baby's equator. "Twenty-three and a half inches," she announced. I was impressed with the way Zenobia's oceans stayed on her surface instead of spilling onto the floor. I hadn't realized anybody that small could have so much gravity.

Now came the big moment. Pam wrapped our baby in a pink receiving blanket and brought her over, and we got our first really good look. Zenobia glowed. She smelled like ozone. She was swaddled in weather—in a wispy coating of clouds and mist. And what lovely mountains we glimpsed through the gaps in her atmosphere, what lush valleys, wondrous deserts, splendid plateaus, radiant lakes.

"She's *beautiful*," said Polly.

"Beautiful," Borealis echoed.

"She's awfully blue," I said. "She getting enough oxygen?"

"I suspect that's normal," said the doctor. "All those oceans . . ."

Instinctively Polly opened her gown and, grasping Zenobia by two opposite archipelagos, pressed the north pole against her flesh. "*Eee-yyyowww,* that's cold," she wailed as the ice cap engulfed her. She pulled our biosphere away, colostrum dribbling from her nipple, her face fixed somewhere between a smile and a wince. "C-cold," she said as she restored Zenobia to her breast. "Brrrr, brrrr . . ."

"She's sucking?" asked Borealis excitedly. "She's actually taking it?"

I'd never seen Polly look happier. "Of *course* she's taking it. These are serious tits I've got. Brrrr . . ."

"This is shaping up to be an extremely weird day," said the assistant surgeon.

"I believe I'm going to be sick," the anesthesiologist announced.

Thinking back, I'm awfully glad I rented an infant car seat from Boalsburg Memorial and took the baby home that night. Sticking Zenobia in the nursery would have been a total disaster, with every gossipmonger and freak seeker in Centre County crowding around as if she were a two-headed calf at the Grange Fair. And I'm convinced that the five days I spent alone with her while Polly mended back at the hospital were vital to our father-daughter bond. Such rosy recollections I have of sitting in the front parlor, Zenobia snugged into the crook of my arm, my body wrapped in a lime-green canvas tarp so her oceans wouldn't soak my shirt; how fondly I remember inserting the nipple of her plastic bottle into the mouthlike depression at her north pole and watching the Similac drain into her axis.

It was tough running the farm without Polly, but my parents pitched in, and even Asa stopped listening to the Apostolic Succession on his CD long enough to help us publish the April *Down to Earth,* the issue urging people to come out and pick their own asparagus. ("And remember, we add the rotenone only after the harvest has stopped, so there's no pesticide residue on the spears themselves.") In the lower right-hand corner we ran a message surrounded by a hot-pink border: WE ARE PLEASED TO ANNOUNCE THE BIRTH OF OUR DAUGHTER, ZENOBIA, A BIOSPHERE, ON MARCH 10TH . . . 9 POUNDS, 6 OUNCES . . . 23½ INCHES.

My parents, God bless them, pretended not to notice Zenobia was the way she was. I still have the patchwork comforter Mom made her, each square showing an exotic animal promoting a different letter of the alphabet: *A* is for Aardvark, *B* is for Bontebok, *Z* is for Zebu. As for Dad, he kept insisting that, when his granddaughter got a bit older, he'd take her fishing on Parson's Pond, stringing her line from the peak of her highest mountain.

According to our child-rearing books, Asa should

have been too mature for anything so crude and uncivil as sibling rivalry; after all, he and Zenobia were over a decade apart—eleven years, two months, and eight days, to be exact. No such luck. I'm thinking, for example, of the time Asa pried up one of Zenobia's glaciers with a shoehorn and used it to cool his root beer. And the time he befouled her Arctic ocean with a can of 3-in-One Lubricating Oil. And, worst of all, the time he shaved off her largest pine barren with a Bic disposable razor. "What the hell do you think you're *doing?*" I shrieked, full blast, which is not one of the responses recommended by Dr. Lionel Dubner in *The Self-Actualized Parent.* "I hate her!" Asa yelled back, a line right out of Dr. Dubner's chapter on Cain and Abel Syndrome. "I hate her, I hate her!"

Even when Zenobia wasn't being abused by her brother, she made a lot of noise—sharp, jagged wails that shot from her fault lines like volcanic debris. Often she became so fussy that nothing would do but for my parents to baby-sit Asa while we took her on a long drive up Route 322 to the top of Mount Skyhook, a windy plateau featuring Jake's Video, an acupuncture clinic, and a chiropodist on one side and the Milky Way Galaxy on the other.

"The minute our Land-Rover pulls within sight of the stars," I wrote in *Down to Earth,* "Zenobia grows calm. We unbuckle her from the car seat," I told our readers, "and set her on the bluff, and immediately she begins rotating on her axis and making contented little clucking sounds, as if she somehow knows the stars are there—as if she senses them with her dark loamy skin."

Years later, I learned to my bewilderment that virtually everyone on our mailing list regarded the Zenobia bulletins in *Down to Earth* as unmitigated put-ons. The customers never believed anything we wrote about our baby, not one word.

Our most memorable visit to Mount Skyhook began with a series of meteor showers. Over and over, bright heavenly droplets shot across the sky, as if old Canis Major had just been given a bath and was shaking himself dry. "Fantastic," I said.

"Exquisite," said Polly.

"Zow-eee," said Zenobia.

My wife and I let out two perfectly synchronized gasps.

"Of course, it's really just junk, isn't it, Mommy?" our baby continued in a reedy and accelerated voice: the voice of an animated raccoon. "Trash from beyond the planets, hitting the air and burning up?"

"You can talk!" gushed Polly.

"I can talk," Zenobia agreed.

"Why didn't you *tell* us?" I demanded.

Our baby spun, showing us the eastern face of her northern hemisphere. "When talking starts, things get . . . well, complicated, right? I prefer simplicity." Zenobia sounded as if she were speaking through an electric fan. "Gosh, but I love it up here. See those stars,

Daddy? They pull at me, know what I mean? They want me."

At which point I noticed my daughter was airborne, floating two feet off the ground like an expiring helium balloon.

"Be careful," I said. "You might . . ."

"What?"

"Fall into the sky."

"You bet, Daddy. I'll be careful." Awash in moonlight, Zenobia's clouds emitted a deep golden glow. Her voice grew soft and dreamy. "The universe, it's a lonely place. It's full of orphans. But the lucky ones find homes." Our baby eased herself back onto the bluff. "I was a lucky one."

"*We* were the lucky ones," said Polly.

"Your mother and I think the world of you," I said.

A sigh escaped from our baby's north pole like water vapor whistling out of a teakettle. "I get so scared sometimes."

"Don't be scared," I said, kicking a rock into the valley.

Zenobia swiveled her Africa equivalent toward Venus. "I keep thinking about . . . history, it's called. Moses' parents, Amram and Jochebed. They took their baby, and they set him adrift." She stopped spinning. Her glaciers sparkled in the moonlight. "I keep thinking about that, and how it was so necessary."

"We'll never set you adrift," said Polly.

"Never," I echoed.

"It was so necessary," said Zenobia in her high, sad voice.

On the evening of Asa's twelfth birthday, Borealis telephoned wanting to know how the baby was doing. I told him she'd reached a circumference of thirty-one inches, but it soon became clear the man wasn't seeking an ordinary chat. He wanted to drop by with Hashigan, Croft, and Logos.

"What'll they do to her?" I asked.

"They'll look at her."

"What else?"

"They'll look, that's all."

I snorted and said, "You'll be just in time for birthday cake," though the fact was I didn't want any of those big shots gawking at our baby, not for a minute.

As it turned out, only Borealis had a piece of Asa's cake. His three pals were hyperserious types, entirely dismayed by the idea of eating from cardboard Apostolic Succession plates. They arrived brimming with tools—with stethoscopes and oscilloscopes, thermometers and spectrometers, with Geiger counters, brainwave monitors, syringes, tweezers, and scalpels. On first seeing Zenobia asleep in her crib, the four doctors gasped in four different registers, like a barbershop quartet experiencing an epiphany.

Hashigan told us Zenobia was "probably the most

important find since the Taung fossil." Croft praised us for keeping the *National Enquirer* and related media out of the picture. Logos insisted that, according to something called the Theory of Transcendental Mutation, a human-gestated biosphere was "bound to appear sooner or later." There was an equation for it.

They poked and probed and prodded our baby; they biopsied her crust. They took water samples, oil specimens, jungle cuttings, and a half-dozen pinches of desert, sealing each trophy in an airtight canister.

"We need to make sure she's not harboring any lethal pathogens," Logos explained.

"She's never even had roseola," Polly replied defensively. "Not even cradle cap."

"Indeed," said Logos, locking my baby's exudations in his briefcase.

"All during this rude assault," I wrote in the November *Down to Earth*, "Zenobia made no sound. I suspect she wants them to think she's just a big dumb rock."

Now that such obviously important folks had shown an interest in our biosphere, Asa's attitude changed. Zenobia was no longer his grotesque little sister. Far from being a bothersome twit, she was potentially the greatest hobby since baseball cards.

All Asa wanted for Christmas was a Johnny Genius Microscope Kit and some theatrical floodlights, and we soon learned why. He suspended the lights over

Zenobia's crib, set up the microscope, and got to work, scrutinizing his baby sister with all the intensity of Louis Pasteur on the trail of rabies. He kept a detailed log of the changes he observed: the exuberant flowering of Zenobia's rain forests, the languid waltz of her continental plates, the ebb and flow of her ice shelves—and, most astonishingly, the abrupt appearance of phosphorescent fish and strange aquatic lizards in her seas.

"She's got fish!" Asa shrieked, running through the house. "Mom! Dad! Zenobia's got lizards and fish!"

"Whether our baby's life-forms have arisen spontaneously," we told the readers of *Down to Earth*, "or through some agency outside her bounds, is a question we are not yet prepared to answer."

Within a month our son had, in true scientific fashion, devised a hypothesis to account for Zenobia's physiognomy. According to Asa, events on his sister were directly connected to the atmosphere around Garber Farm.

And he was right. Whenever Polly and I allowed one of our quarrels to degenerate into cold silence, Zenobia's fish stopped flashing and her glaciers migrated toward her equator. Whenever our dicey finances plunged us into a dark mood, a cloak of moist, gray fog would enshroud Zenobia for hours. Angry words, such as Polly and I employed in persuading Asa to clean up his room, made our baby's oceans bubble and seethe like abandoned soup on a hot stove.

"For Zenobia's sake, we've resolved to keep our household as tranquil as possible," we wrote in *Down to Earth*. "We've promised to be nice to each other. It seems immoral, somehow, to bind a biosphere to anything so chancy as the emotional ups and downs of an American family."

Although we should have interpreted our daughter's fish and lizards as harbingers of things to come, the arrival of the dinosaurs still took us by surprise. But there they were, actual Jurassic dinosaurs, thousands of them, galumphing around on Zenobia like she was a remake of *King Kong*. How we loved to watch the primordial drama now unfolding at the far end of Asa's microscope: fierce tyrannosaurs pouncing on their prey, flocks of pterodactyls floating through her troposphere like organic 747s (though they were not truly dinosaurs, Asa explained), herds of amiable duckbills sauntering through our baby's marshes. This was the supreme science project, the ultimate electric train set, a flea circus directed by Cecil B. DeMille.

"I'm worried about her," Asa told me a month after Zenobia's dinosaurs evolved. "The pH of her precipitation is 4.2 when it should be 5.6."

"Huh?"

"It should be 5.6."

"What are you talking about?"

"I'm talking about acid rain, Dad. I'm talking about Zenobia's lakes becoming as dead as the moon."

"Acid rain?" I said. "How could that be? She doesn't even have people."

"I know, Dad, but *we* do."

"Sad news," I wrote in *Down to Earth*. "Maybe if Asa hadn't been away at computer camp, things would have gone differently."

It was the Fourth of July. We'd invited a bunch of families over for a combination potluck supper and volleyball tournament in the north pasture, and the farm was soon swarming with bored, itchy children. I suspect that a gang of them wandered into the baby's room and, mistaking her for some sort of toy, carried her outside. At this point, evidently, the children got an idea. A foolish, perverse, wicked idea.

They decided to take Zenobia into the basset barn.

The awful noise—a blend of kids laughing, hounds baying, and a biosphere screaming—brought Polly and me on the run. My first impression was of some bizarre and incomprehensible athletic event, a sport played in hell or in the fantasies of an opium eater. Then I saw the truth: the dogs had captured our daughter. Yes, there they were, five bitches and a dozen pups, clumsily batting her around the barn with their snouts, oafishly pinning her under their paws. They scratched her ice caps, chewed on her islands, lapped up her oceans.

"Daddy, get them off me!" Zenobia cried, rolling amid the clouds of dust and straw. "Get them off!"

"Help her!" screamed Polly.

"Mommy! Daddy!"

I jumped into the drooling dogpile, punching the animals in their noses, knocking them aside with my knees. Somehow I got my hands around our baby's equator, and with a sudden tug I freed her from the mass of soggy fur and slavering tongues. Pressing her against my chest, I ran blindly from the barn.

Tooth marks dotted Zenobia's terrain like meteor craters. Her largest continent was fractured in five places. Her crust leaked crude oil, her mountains vomited lava.

But the worst of it was our daughter's unshakable realization that a great loss had occurred. "Where are my dinosaurs?" she shrieked. "I can't feel my dinosaurs!"

"There, there, Zenobia," I said.

"They'll be okay," said Polly.

"They're g-gone," wailed Zenobia. "Oh, dear, oh, dear, they're *gone!*"

I rushed our baby into the nursery and positioned her under Asa's rig. An extinction: true, all horribly true. Zenobia's swamps were empty; her savannas were bereft of prehistoric life; not a single vertebrate scurried through her forests.

She was inconsolable. "My apatosaurs," she groaned. "Where are my apatosaurs? Where *are* they?"

Mowed down, pulverized, flung into space.

"There, there, darling," said Polly. "There, there."

"I want them back."

"There, there," said Polly.

"I miss them."

"There, there."

"Make them come back."

The night Asa returned from camp, Borealis and his buddy Logos dropped by, just in time for a slice of Garber Farm's famous raspberry pie. Borealis looked sheepish and fretful. "My friend has something to tell you," he said. "A kind of proposal."

Having consumed an entire jar of Beech-Nut strained sweet potatoes and two bottles of Similac, the baby was in bed for the night. Her flutelike snores wafted into the kitchen as Polly and Asa served our guests.

Logos sat down, resting his spindly hands on the red-and-white checkerboard oilcloth as if trying to levitate the table. "Ben, Polly, I'll begin by saying I'm not a religious man. Not the sort of man who's inclined to believe in God. But . . ."

"Yes?" said Polly, raising her eyebrows in a frank display of mistrust.

"But I can't shake my conviction that your Zenobia has been · . . . well, sent. I feel that Providence has deposited her in our laps."

"She was deposited in my lap," Polly corrected him. "My lap and Ben's."

"I think it was the progesterone suppositories," I said.

"Did you ever hear how, in the old days, coal miners used to take canaries down into the shaft with them?"

asked Logos, forking a gluey clump of raspberries into his mouth. "When the canary started squawking, or stopped singing, or fell to the bottom of the cage and died, the men knew poison gases were leaking into the mine." The health commissioner devoured his pie slice in a half-dozen bites. "Well, Ben and Polly, it seems to me that your Zenobia is like that. It seems to me God has given us a canary."

"She's a biosphere," said Asa.

Without asking, Logos slashed into the remaining pie, excising a fresh piece. "I've been on the horn to Washington all week, and I must say the news is very, very good. Ready, Ben—ready, Polly?" The commissioner cast a twinkling eye on our boy. "Ready, son? Get this." He gestured as if fanning open a stack of money. "The Department of the Interior is prepared to pay you three hundred thousand dollars—that's three hundred thousand, cash—for Zenobia."

"What are you talking about?" I asked.

"I'm talking about buying that little canary of yours for three hundred thousand bucks."

"*Buying her?*" said my wife, inflating. Polly the puff adder, Polly the randy tree frog.

"She's the environmental simulacrum we've always wanted," said Logos. "With Zenobia, we can convincingly model the long-term effects of fluorocarbons, nitrous oxide, mercury, methane, chlorine, and lead. For the first time, we can study the impact of deforestation and ozone depletion without ever leaving the lab."

Polly and I stared at each other, making vows with our eyes. We were patriotic Americans, my wife and me, but nobody was going to deplete our baby's ozone, not even the President of the United States himself.

"Look at it this way," said Borealis; he gripped his coffee mug with one hand, tugged anxiously at the kitchen curtains with the other. "If scientists can finally offer an irrefutable scenario of ecological collapse, then the world's governments may really start listening, and Asa here will get to grow up on a safer, cleaner planet. Everybody benefits."

"Zenobia doesn't benefit," said Polly.

Borealis slurped coffee. "Yes, but there's a greater good here, right, folks?"

"She's just a *globe,* for Christ's sake," said Logos.

"She's our globe," I said.

"Our baby," said Polly.

"My sister," said Asa.

Logos massaged his beard. "Look, I hate to play hardball with nice people like you, but you don't really have a choice here. Our test results are in, and the fact is your biosphere harbors a maverick form of the simian T-lymphotrophic retrovirus. As county health commissioner, I have the authority to remove the creature from these premises forthwith and quarantine it."

" 'The fact is,' " I snorted, echoing Logos. " 'The fact is'—*the fact is,* our baby couldn't give my great aunt Jennifer a bad cold." I shot a glance at Borealis. "Am I right?"

The doctor said, "Well . . ."

Logos grunted like one of the pigs we used to raise before the market went soft.

"I think you gentlemen had better leave," my wife suggested icily.

"We have a barnful of *dogs,*" said Asa in a tone at once cheerful and menacing. "Mean ones," he added with a quick little nod.

"I'll be back," said the commissioner, rising. "Tomorrow. And I won't be alone."

"Bastard," said Polly—the first time I'd ever heard her use that word.

So we did what we had to do; like Amram and Jochebed, we did what was necessary. Polly drove. I brooded. All the way up Route 322, Zenobia sat motionless in the back, safely buckled into her car seat, moaning and whimpering. Occasionally Asa leaned over and gently ran his hairbrush through the jungles of her southern hemisphere.

"Gorgeous sky tonight," I observed, unhooking our baby and carrying her into the crisp September darkness.

"I see that." Zenobia fought to keep her voice in one piece.

"I hate this," I said, marching toward the bluff. My guts were as cold and hard as one of Zenobia's glaciers. "Hate it, hate it . . ."

"It's necessary," she said.

We spent the next twenty minutes picking out constellations. Brave Orion; royal Cassiopeia; snarly old Ursa Minor; the Big Dipper with its bowlful of galactic dust. Asa stayed by the Land-Rover, digging his heel into the dirt and refusing to join us, even though he knew ten times more astronomy than the rest of us.

"Let's get it over with," said our baby.

"No," said Polly. "We have all night."

"It won't be any easier in an hour."

"Let me hold her," said Asa, shuffling onto the bluff.

He took his sister, raised her toward the flickering sky. He whispered to her—statistical bits that made no sense to me, odd talk of sea levels, hydrogen ions, and solar infrared. I passed the time staring at Jake's Video, its windows papered with ads for Joe Dante's remake of *The War of the Worlds*.

The boy choked down a sob. "Here," he said, pivoting toward me. "You do it."

Gently I slid the biosphere from my son. Hugging Zenobia tightly, I kissed her most arid desert as Polly stroked her equator. Zenobia wept, her arroyos, wadis, and floodplains filling with tears. I stretched out my arms as far as they would go, lifting our daughter high above my head.

Once and only once in my days on the courts did I ever hit a three-pointer.

"We'll miss you," I told Zenobia. She felt weightless, airy, as if she were a hollow glass ornament from a Garber Farm Christmas tree. It was just as she'd said: the stars wanted her. They tugged at her blood.

"We love you," groaned Polly.

"Daddy!" Zenobia called from her lofty perch. Her tears splashed my face like raindrops. "Mommy!" she wailed. "Asa!"

In a quick, flashy spasm I made my throw. A good one—straight and smooth. Zenobia flew soundlessly from my fingertips.

"Bye-bye!" the three of us shouted as she soared into the bright, beckoning night. We waved furiously, maniacally, as if hoping to generate enough turbulence to pull her back to central Pennsylvania. "Bye-bye, Zenobia!"

"Bye-bye!" our baby called from out of the speckled darkness, and then she was gone.

The Earth turned—once, twice. Raspberries, apples, Christmas trees, asparagus, basset pups—each crop made its demands, and by staying busy we stayed sane.

One morning during the height of raspberry season I was supervising our roadside fruit stand and chatting with one of our regulars—Lucy Berens, Asa's former third-grade teacher—when Polly rushed over. She looked crazed and pleased. Her eyes expanded like domes of bubble gum emerging from Asa's mouth.

She told me she'd just tried printing out a *Down to Earth,* only the ImageWriter II had delivered something else entirely. "Here," she said, shoving a piece of computer paper in my face, its edges embroidered with sprocket holes.

Dear Mom and Dad:

This is being transmitted via a superluminal wave generated by nonlocal quantum correlations. You won't be able to write back.

I have finally found a proper place for myself, ten light-years from Garber Farm. In my winter, I can see your star. Your system is part of a constellation that looks to me like a Zebu. Z is for Zebu, remember? I am happy.

Big news. A year ago, various mammalian lines—tree shrews, mostly—emerged from those few feeble survivors of the Fourth of July catastrophe. And then, last month, I acquired—are you ready?—people. That's right, people. Human beings, sentient primates, creatures entirely like yourselves. God, but they're clever: cars, deodorants, polyvinyl chlorides, all of it. I like them. They're brighter than the dinosaurs, and they have a certain spirituality. In short, they're almost worthy of being what they are: your grandchildren.

Every day, my people look out across the heavens, and their collective gaze comes to rest on Earth. Thanks to Asa, I can explain to them what they're seeing, all the folly and waste, the way your whole planet's becoming a cesspool. So tell my brother he has saved my life. And tell him to study hard—he'll be a great scientist when he grows up.

Mom and Dad, I think of you every day. I hope you're doing well, and that Garber Farm is prospering. Give Asa a kiss for me.

All my love,
Zenobia

"A letter from our daughter," I explained to Lucy Berens.

"Didn't know you had one," said Lucy, snatching up an aluminum pail so she could go pick a quart of raspberries.

"She's far away," said Polly.

"She's happy," I said.

That night, we went into Asa's room while he was practicing on his trap set, thumping along with the Apostolic Succession. He shut off the CD, put down his drumsticks, and read Zenobia's letter—slowly, solemnly. He yawned and slipped the letter into his math book. He told us he was going to bed. Fourteen: a moody age.

"You saved her life?" I said. "What does she mean?"

"You don't get it?"

"Uh-uh."

Our son drummed a paradiddle on his math book. "Remember what Dr. Logos said about those coal miners? Remember when he told us Zenobia was like a canary? Well, obviously he got it backwards. My sister's not the canary—*we* are. *Earth* is."

"Huh?" said Polly.

"We're Zenobia's canary," said Asa.

We kissed our son, left his room, closed the door. The hallway was papered over with his treasures—with MISS PIGGY FOR PRESIDENT posters, rock star portraits, and lobby cards from the various environmental apocalypses he'd been renting regularly from Jake's Video: *Silent Running, Soylent Green, Frogs . . .*

"We're Zenobia's canary," said Polly.

"Is it too late for us, then?" I asked.

My wife didn't answer.

You've heard the rest. How Dr. Borealis knew somebody who knew somebody, and suddenly we were seeing Senator Caracalla on C-Span, reading the last twelve issues of *Down to Earth,* the whole story of Zenobia's year among us, into the *Congressional Record.*

Remember what President Tait told the newspapers the day he signed the Caracalla Conservation Act into law? "Sometimes all you need is a pertinent parable," he said. "Sometimes all you need is the right metaphor," our chief executive informed us.

The Earth is not our mother.

Quite the opposite.

That particular night, however, standing outside Asa's room, Polly and I weren't thinking about metaphors. We were thinking about how much we wanted Zenobia back. We're pretty good parents, Polly and I. Look at our kids.

We winked at each other, tiptoed down the hall, and climbed into bed. Our bodies pressed together, and we laughed out loud. I've always loved my wife's smell; she's like some big floppy mushroom you came across in the woods when you were six years old, all sweet and damp and forbidden. We kept on pressing, and it kept feeling better and better. We were hoping for another girl.

Known But to God and Wilbur Hines

❖

MY KEEPER faces east, his gaze lifting above the treetops and traveling across the national necropolis clear to the glassy Potomac. His bayonet rises into the morning sky, as if to skewer the sun. In his mind he ticks off the seconds, one for each shell in a twenty-one-gun salute.

Being dead has its advantages. True, my pickled flesh is locked away inside this cold marble box, but my senses float free, as if they were orbiting satellites beaming back snippets of the world. I see the city, dense with black citizens and white marble. I smell the Virginia air, the ripe grass, the river's scum. I hear my keeper's boots as he pivots south, the echo of his heels coming together: two clicks, always two, like a telegrapher transmitting an eternal *I*.

My keeper pretends not to notice the crowd—the fifth graders, Rotarians, garden clubbers, random tourists. Occasionally he catches a cub scout's bright yellow bandanna or a punker's pink mohawk. "Known but to God," it says on my tomb. Not true, for I'm known to myself as well. I understand Wilbur Simpson Hines perfectly.

Thock, thock, thock goes my keeper's Springfield as he transfers it from his left shoulder to his right. He pauses, twenty-one seconds again, then marches south twenty-one paces down the narrow black path, protecting me from the Bethesda Golden Age Society and the Glen Echo Lions Club.

I joined the army to learn how to kill my father. An irony: the only time the old man ever showed a glimmer of satisfaction with me occurred when I announced I was dropping out of college and enlisting. He thought I wanted to make the world safe for democracy, when in fact I wanted to make it safe from him. I intended to sign up under a false name. Become competent with a rifle. Then one night, while my father slept, I would sneak away from basic training, press the muzzle to his head—Harry Hines the hot-blooded Pennsylvania farmer, laying into me with his divining rod till my back was freckled with slivers of hazelwood—and blow him straight to Satan's backyard. You see how irrational I was in those days? The tomb has smoothed me out. There's no treatment like this box, no therapy like death.

Click, click, my keeper faces east. He pauses for twenty-one seconds, watching the morning mist hovering above the river.

"I want to be a doughboy," I told them at the Boals-burg Recruiting Station. They parceled me. Name: Bill Johnson. Address: Bellefonte YMCA. Complexion: fair. Eye color: blue. Hair: red.

"Get on the scales," they said.

They measured me, and for a few dicey minutes I feared that, being short and scrawny—my father always detested the fact that I wasn't a gorilla like him—I'd flunk out, but the sergeant just winked at me and said, "Stand on our toes, Bill."

I did, stretching to the minimum height.

"You probably skipped breakfast this morning, right?" said the sergeant. Another wink. "Breakfast is good for a few pounds."

"Yes, sir."

My keeper turns: click, click, left face. Thock, thock, thock, he transfers his rifle from his right shoulder to his left. He pauses for twenty-one seconds then marches north down the black path. Click, click, he spins toward the Potomac and waits.

It's hard to say exactly why my plans changed. At Camp Sinclair they put me in a crisp khaki uniform and gave me a mess kit, a canteen, and a Remington rifle, and suddenly there I was, Private Bill Johnson of the American Expeditionary Forces, D Company, Eighteenth U.S. Infantry, First Division. And, of course, everybody was saying what a great time we were going to have driving the Heinies into the Baltic and seeing gay Paree. The Yanks were coming, and I wanted to be one of them—Bill Johnson née Wilbur Hines wasn't about to risk an AWOL conviction and a tour in the brig while his friends were off visiting *la belle France* and its French belles. After my discharge, there'd be plenty of time to show Harry Hines what his son had learned in the army.

They're changing the guard. For the next half hour, an African-American PFC will protect me. We used to call them coloreds, of course. Niggers, to tell you the truth. Today this particular African-American has a fancy job patrolling my tomb, but when they laid me here in 1921 his people weren't even allowed in the regular divisions. The 365th, that was the nigger regiment, and when they finally reached France, you know what Pershing had them do? Dig trenches, unload ships, and bury white doughboys.

But my division—*we'd* get a crack at glory, oh, yes. They shipped us over on the British tub *Magnolia* and dropped us down near the front line a mile west of a jerkwater Frog village, General Robert Bullard in charge. I'm not sure what I expected from France. My buddy Alvin Platt said they'd fill our canteens with red wine every morning. They didn't. Somehow I thought I'd be in the war without actually *fighting* the war, but suddenly there we were, sharing a four-foot trench with a million cooties and dodging *Mieniewaffers* like some idiots you'd see in a newsreel at the Ziegfeld with a Fairbanks picture and a Chaplin two-reeler, everybody listening for the dreaded cry "Gas attack!" and waiting for the order to move forward. By April of 1918 we'd all seen enough victims of Boche mustard—coughing up blood, shitting their gizzards out, weeping from blind eyes—that we clung to our gas masks like little boys hugging their teddies.

My keeper marches south, his bayonet cutting a straight incision in the summer air. I wonder if he's ever used it. Probably not. I used mine plenty in '18. "If a Heinie comes toward you with his hands up yelling 'Kamerad,' don't be fooled," Sergeant Fiskejohn told us back at Camp Sinclair. "He's sure as hell got a potato masher in one of those hands. Go at him from below, and you'll stop him easy. A long thrust in the belly, then a short one, then a butt stroke to the chin if he's still on his feet, which he won't be."

On May 28 the order came through, and we climbed out of the trenches and fought what's now called the Battle of Cantigny, but it wasn't really a battle, it was a grinding push into the German salient with hundreds of men on both sides getting hacked to bits like we were a bunch of steer haunches hanging in our barns back home. Evidently the Boche caught more than we did, because after forty-five minutes that town was ours, and we waltzed down the gunky streets singing our favorite ditty.

The mademoiselle from gay Paree, parlez-vous?
The mademoiselle from gay Paree, parlez-vous?

The mademoiselle from gay Paree,
She had the clap and she gave it to me,
Hinky Dinky, parlez-vous?

I'll never forget the first time I drew a bead on a Heinie, a sergeant with a handlebar mustache flaring from his upper lip like antlers. I aimed, I squeezed, I killed him, just like that: now he's up, now he's down—a man I didn't even know. I thought how easy it was going to be shooting Harry Hines, a man I hated.

For the next three days the Boche counterattacked, and then I did learn to hate them. Whenever somebody lost an arm or a leg to a potato masher, he'd cry for his mother, in English mostly but sometimes in Spanish and sometimes Yiddish, and you can't see that happen more than once without wanting to kill every Heinie in Europe, right up to the Kaiser himself. I did as Fiskejohn said. A boy would stumble toward me with his hands up—*"Kamerad! Kamerad!"*—and I'd go for his belly. There's something about having a Remington in your grasp with that lovely slice of steel jutting from the bore. I'd open the fellow up left to right, like I was underlining a passage in the sharpshooter's manual, and he'd spill out like soup. It was interesting and legal. Once I saw a sardine. On the whole, though, Fiskejohn was wrong. The dozen boys I ripped weren't holding potato mashers or anything else.

I switched tactics. I took prisoners. *"Kamerad!"* Five at first. *"Kamerad!"* Six. *"Kamerad!"* Seven. Except that seventh boy in fact had a masher, which he promptly lobbed into my chest.

Lucky for me, it bounced back.

The Heinie caught enough of the kick to get his face torn off, whereas I caught only enough to earn myself a bed in the field hospital. For a minute I didn't know I was wounded. I just looked at that boy who had no nose, no lower jaw, and wondered whether perhaps I should use a grenade on Harry Hines.

Click, click, my keeper turns to the left. Thock, thock, thock, he transfers his rifle, waits. The Old Guard—the Third U.S. Infantry—never quits. Twenty-four hours a day, seven days a week: can you imagine? Three A.M. on Christmas morning, say, with snow tumbling down and nobody around except a lot of dead veterans, and here's this grim, silent sentinel strutting past my tomb? It gives me the creeps.

The division surgeons spliced me together as best they could, but I knew they'd left some chips behind because my chest hurt like hell. A week after I was taken off the critical list, they gave me a month's pay and sent me to Bar-le-Duc for some rest and relaxation, which everybody knew meant cognac and whores.

The whole village was a red-light district, and if you had the francs you could find love around the clock, though you'd do well to study the choices and see who had that itchy look a lady acquires when she's got the clap. And so it was that on the first of July, as the hot French twilight poured into a cootie-ridden bordello on the Place Vendôme, Wilbur Hines's willy finally put to port after nineteen years at sea. Like Cantigny, it was quick and confusing and over before I knew it. I had six more days coming to me, though, and I figured it would get better.

My keeper heads north, twenty-one paces. The sun beats down. The sweatband of his cap is rank and soggy. Click, click: right face. His eyes lock on the river.

I loved Bar-le-Duc. The citizens treated me like a war hero, saluting me wherever I went. There's no telling how far you'll go in this world if you're willing to belly-rip a few German teenagers.

Beyond the Poilu and the hookers, the cafés were also swarming with Bolsheviks, and I must admit their ideas made sense to me—at least, they did by my fourth glass of Château d'Yquem. After Cantigny, with its flying metal and Alvin Platt walking around with a bloody stump screaming "Mommy!" I'd begun asking the same questions as the Bolshies, such as, "Why are we having this war, anyway?" When I told them my family was poor, the Bolshies got all excited, and I hadn't felt so important since the army took me. I actually gave those fellows a few francs, and they promptly signed me up as a noncom in their organization. So now I held two ranks, PFC in the American Expeditionary Forces and lance corporal in the International Brotherhood of Proletarian Veterans or whatever the hell they were calling themselves.

My third night on the cathouse circuit, I got into an

argument with one of the tarts. Fifi—I always called them Fifi—decided she'd given me special treatment on our second round, something to do with her mouth, her *bouche,* and now she wanted twenty francs instead of the usual ten. Those ladies thought every doughboy was made of money. All you heard in Bar-le-Duc was *"les Americains, beaucoup d'argent."*

"Dix francs," I said.

"Vingt," Fifi insisted. Her eyes looked like two dead snails. Her hair was the color of Holstein dung.

"Dix."

"Vingt—or I tell ze MP you rip me," Fifi threatened. She meant rape.

"Dix," I said, throwing the coins on the bed, whereupon Fifi announced with a tilted smile that she had "a bad case of ze VD" and hoped she'd given it to me.

Just remember, you weren't there. Your body wasn't full of raw metal, and you didn't have Fifi's clap, and nobody was expecting you to maintain a lot of distinctions between the surrendering boys you were supposed to stab and the Frog tarts you weren't. It was hot. My chest hurt. Half my friends had died capturing a pissant hamlet whose streets were made of horse manure. And all I could see were those nasty little clap germs gnawing at my favorite organs.

My Remington stood by the door. The bayonet was tinted now, the color of a turnip; so different from the war itself, that bayonet—no question about its purpose. As I pushed it into Fifi and listened to the rasp of the steel against her pelvis, I thought how prophetic her mis-pronunciation had been: I tell ze MP you rip me.

I used the fire escape. My hands were wet and warm. All the way back to my room, I felt a gnawing in my gut like I'd been gassed. I wished I'd never stood on my toes in the Boalsburg Recruiting Station. A ditty helped. After six reprises and a bottle of cognac, I finally fell asleep.

> *The mademoiselle from Bar-le-Duc, parlez-vous?*
> *The mademoiselle from Bar-le-Duc, parlez-vous?*
> *The mademoiselle from Bar-le-Duc,*
> *She'll screw you in the chicken coop,*
> *Hinky Dinky, parlez-vous?*

On the sixteenth of July, I boarded one of those 40-and-8 trains and rejoined my regiment, now dug in along the Marne. A big fight had already happened there, sometime in '14, and they were hoping for another. I was actually glad to be leaving Bar-le-Duc, for all its wonders and delights. The local gendarmes, I'd heard, were look-ing into the Fifi matter.

Click, click, thock, thock, thock. My keeper pauses, twenty-one seconds. He marches south down the black path.

At the Marne they put me in charge of a Hotchkiss machine gun, and I set it up on a muddy hill, the better to cover the forward trench where they'd stationed my platoon. I had two good friends in that hole, and so when Captain Mallery showed up with orders from *le général*—we were now part of the XX French Corps—

saying I should haul the Hotchkiss a mile downstream, I went berserk.

"Those boys are completely exposed," I protested. The junk in my chest was on fire. "If there's an infantry attack, we'll lose 'em all."

"Move the Hotchkiss, Private Johnson," the captain said.

"That's not a very good idea," I said.

"Move it."

"They'll be naked as jaybirds."

"Move it. *Now.*"

A couple of wars later, of course, attacks on officers by their own men got raised to a kind of art form— I know all about it, I like to read the tourists' newspapers—but this was 1918 and the concept was still in its infancy. I certainly didn't display much finesse as I pulled out my Colt revolver and in a pioneering effort shot Mallery through the heart. It was all pretty crude.

And then, damn, who should happen by but the CO himself, crusty old Colonel Horrocks, his eyes bulging with disbelief. He told me I was arrested. He said I'd hang. But by then I was fed up. I was fed up with gas scares and Alvin Platt getting his arm blown off. I was fed up with being an American infantry private and an honorary Bolshevik, fed up with greedy hookers and gonorrhea and the whole dumb, bloody, smelly war. So I ran. That's right: ran, retreated, quit the western front.

Unfortunately, I picked the wrong direction. I'd meant to make my way into Château-Thierry and hide out in the cathouses till the Mallery situation blew over, but instead I found myself heading toward Deutschland itself, oh, yes, straight for the enemy line. Stupid, stupid.

When I saw my error, I threw up my hands.

And screamed.

"Kamerad! Kamerad!"

Bill Johnson née Wilbur Hines never fought in the Second Battle of the Marne. He never helped his regiment drive the Heinies back eight miles, capture four thousand of the Kaiser's best troops, and kill God knows how many more. This private missed it all, because the Boche hit him with everything they had. Machine-gun fire, grapeshot, rifle bullets, shrapnel. A potato masher detonated. A mustard shell went off. Name: unknown. Address: unknown. Complexion: charred. Eye color: no eyes. Hair: burned off. Weeks later, when they scraped me off the Marne floodplain, it was obvious I was a prime candidate for the Arlington program. Lucky for me, Colonel Horrocks got killed at Soissons. He'd have voted me down.

As I said, I read the newspapers. I keep up. That's how I learned about my father. One week after they put me in this box, Harry Hines cheated at seven-card stud and was bludgeoned to death by the loser with a ball peen hammer. It made the front page of the *Centre County Democrat*.

It's raining. The old people hoist their umbrellas; the fifth graders glom onto their teacher; the cub scouts march away like a platoon of midgets. Am I angry about my life? For many years, yes, I was furious, but then the eighties rolled around, mine and the century's, and I realized I'd be dead by now anyway. So I won't leave you with any bitter thoughts. I'll leave you with a pretty song.

Listen.

> *The mademoiselle from Is-sur-Tille, parlez-vous?*
> *The mademoiselle from Is-sur-Tille, parlez-vous?*
> *The mademoiselle from Is-sur-Tille,*
> *She can zig-zig-zig like a spinning wheel,*
> *Hinky Dinky, parlez-vous?*

My keeper remains, facing east.

Bible Stories for Adults, No. 20: The Tower

❖

BEING GOD, I must choose My words carefully. People, I've noticed, tend to hang on to My every remark. It gets annoying, this servile and sycophantic streak in *Homo sapiens sapiens*. There's a difference, after all, between tasteful adulation and arrant toadyism, but they just don't get it.

I've always thought of Myself as a kind of parent. God the Father and all that. But an effective mom, dad, or Supreme Being is not necessarily a permissive mom, dad, or Supreme Being. Spare the rod, and you'll spoil the species. Sometimes it's best to be strict.

Was I too strict with Daniel Nimrod? Did I judge the man too harshly? My angels don't think so; they believe his overbearing vanity—Nimrod the enfant terrible of American real estate, slapping his name on everything from Atlantic City casinos to San Francisco condos—

merited the very comeuppance he received. Hear My tale.
Decide for yourself. I shall say this. As divine retributions
go, it was surely My most creative work since the locusts,
lice, flies, murrain, blood, boils, dead children, hail,
frogs, and darkness. And here's the kicker, people: I did
it with language alone.

As I said, I must choose My words carefully.

We all must.

Listen.

Like so many things in Michael Prete's safe, comfortable,
and unenviable life, this began with the telephone. A
crank call, he naturally assumed. Not that he was an
atheist, nor even an agnostic. He attended Mass regularly. He voted for Republicans. But when a person rings
you up claiming to be God Almighty, you are not automatically inclined to believe him.

There were ambiguities, though. For one thing, the
call had come through on the private phone in Michael's
bedroom and not on the corporation line in his study.
(How could a common lunatic have acquired those seven
heavily guarded digits?) For another, the caller was
claiming to be the very same anonymous eccentric who,
back in '83, had agreed to pay out twelve thousand dollars, twelve times a year, for the privilege of occupying
the Nimrod Tower penthouse. The man had actually
raised the rent on himself: an additional thousand a
month, provided he could move in immediately, even

though the Tower atrium was still festooned with scaffolding and cloaked in plywood panels.

"Come to the penthouse," the mystery voice told Michael upon identifying himself as the Lord God of Hosts, the King of the Universe, the Architect of Reality, the Supreme Being, and so on. "Nine P.M. sharp." The voice was high, brittle, and cosmopolitan, suffused with the accentless accent of the excessively educated. "We must talk, you and I."

"About what?"

"Your boss," the voice replied. "You know more about Daniel Nimrod than does anyone else on the planet, including that overdressed mistress of his. There's quite a lot at stake here: the destiny of the earth, the future of humankind, things like that. Bring a calendar."

"If you're really who you say you are," ventured Michael, intent on catching the crank in a manifest lapse of logic, "why are you living in Nimrod Tower?"

"You think God Almighty should be living in a lousy Holiday Inn? What kind of jerk do you think I am? Nine P.M. sharp. So long."

Michael slipped into the green velvet suit he'd recently purchased at Napoleon's, snatched up his Spanish-leather valise from Loewe's, and descended fifteen floors to street level. Within seconds a Yellow Cab, dome lit, came rattling down Lexington Avenue, pushing through the squalls of snow. (Every year at this time, the same idea haunted Michael: I deserve my own chauffeur—I've earned it.) He flagged down the taxi and climbed into the cozy interior, its seats redolent of oiled leather and surreptitious sex. "Nimrod Tower," he told the driver, a Rastafarian with a knitted cap and gold tooth. "Fifth Avenue and—"

"I *know* where it is, mon—why else you fine folks be paying me, if not to know? Why else you be giving me such a fat and juicy tip on top?"

They crossed Madison, swung left onto Fifth. February already, but the city still seemed Christmasy: the red and green of the traffic lights, the swirling snow. At Fifty-sixth the Jamaican pulled over. "Door to door, eh, mon?" he said cheerfully, musically. Michael paid the $9.50 on the meter, adding a generous three-dollar gratuity.

He recognized the security force immediately, Manuel and George, the former a tall, spindly, grim Puerto Rican who spoke no English, the latter a self-confident and raffish African-American, both wearing the gaudy crimson tunics Mrs. Nimrod had imported from Baghdad. By day the Tower's guards functioned mainly as treats for the tourists, a touch of the Arabian Nights in midtown Manhattan, but after eight the show ended, and any underclass scum attempting to breach the skyscraper quickly discovered that these men were real guards equipped with genuine guns.

"*Buenas noches,* Señor Prete," said Manuel morosely, his pith helmet shining in the roseate light spilling from the atrium.

"What's new with the Poobah?" asked George, grimacing. A two-foot-high bearskin busby sat atop his head like a treed possum.

"He's in Japan," said Michael.

"Buying it?" asked George, sniggering.

"Not exactly," said Michael, for it was merely the Island of Yaku Shima that Mr. Nimrod intended to buy.

Michael entered the atrium—a dazzling space, epic, echoey, and grand, agleam with polished bronze trimmings and florid Breccia Perniche marble. Boarding the escalator, he ascended though the tiers of polyglot shops. Level A, Loewe's of Spain; Level B, Jourdan's of France; Level C, Beck's of Germany; Level D, Pineider's of Italy. Michael's own stooped self glided by, caught in a gleaming copper panel—his hunched shoulders, receding hairline, pinched sad-eyed face. He got off on E, the floor from which the multispeed, indoor waterfall, at the moment set on Slow, commenced its perpetual plunge. Marching past Norman Crider Antiques, he flashed his corporation pass to the Vietnamese guard and stepped into the open elevator.

The penthouse commanded the entire sixty-third floor. A castle in the clouds, Michael mused as he rose, his eardrums tightening with the force of his ascent; a San Simeon of the sky, he decided, disembarking. The front door, a slab of glossy oak, held a bronze ring threaded through the nostrils of a minotaur. He grasped the ring and knocked.

God answered. At least, that was who the penthouse's occupant claimed to be. "Hi, I'm God," he said amiably, "into macroevolution, quantum mechanics, and Jewish history." Those cosmopolitan tones again, filtered this time through the pressure in Michael's ears.

"Michael Prete."

"I know," said the alleged deity. "Everything," he added. With his dusky skin, Prince Valiant haircut, and deep chocolate eyes, he seemed of no particular nationality, and his age and gender were likewise indeterminate. A mildly feminine bosom swelled the breast of his white silk housecoat.

They shook hands.

"I suppose you'd like some sort of proof," said the penthouse's owner in a subtly chiding voice. He led Michael into a parlor paved with carpeting so soft and thick it was like walking on a gigantic pat of butter. "I suppose you expect a sign." They moved past a Steinway grand piano to a tract of window the size of a squash court. *"Viola,"* said the rich man, gesturing toward the storm-swept city below.

Being God, I was able to give Michael Prete several signs that night. First I made the blizzard disappear. *Whoosh, poof,* and suddenly it was a sweltering summer night in New York, not a smidgen of slush, not one snowflake. The thermometer read ninety-one degrees Fahrenheit.

Michael was impressed, but his skepticism vanished completely only after I filled the nocturnal sky with phosphorescent seraphim singing "A Mighty Fortress Is Our

God" and the streets with platoons of cherubim giving out roast turkeys to homeless alcoholics.

I changed everything back, of course. Restored the season, recalled the turkeys, sent the angels home, wiped all trace of the event from the collective consciousness. If You intervene too profusely in Earth's affairs, I've noticed, the inhabitants become chronically distracted, and they forget to worship You.

"Would you like a drink?"

"Y-yes. A d-drink. Please." Michael was so shaken he'd dropped his Spanish-leather valise on the rug. "Are You really *God*? God Himself?"

"Ever since I can remember."

"This is hard to take. You can understand that, right? Do You have any brandy, God, Sir?"

The Almighty strolled to His mahogany bookshelves and took down two sparkling cognac glasses and a crystalline decanter containing a honey-colored liquid. "I want you to come clean about something. A confession, if you will. Given that you're a practicing Catholic, perhaps I should summon a priest . . ."

"Depends on the sin," Michael mumbled, glumly pondering the possibility that he had lost his mind. "If it's venial—"

"You hate Daniel Nimrod, don't you?" God asked abruptly as He filled both glasses with brandy.

Michael gasped so profoundly his clogged ears popped. "It's not a bad situation, this life of mine.

Really. Yes. I've got my own apartment on Lexington with a dishwasher and a rear-screen TV."

"He makes you call him 'sir.' "

"He doesn't *make* me."

"He sounds pompous."

Michael sipped cognac. "Anybody who's achieved as much as Mr. Nimrod—a person like that has a right to be keen on himself, don't You think?"

"You're envious. Your insides are bright green, I can see them. He's got his yacht and his concubines and his name in *Fortune* every month, and what have you got, Prete? You can't even get a *date*. Never mind. We'll change the subject. What can you tell me about Nimrod Gorge?"

Michael knotted up; he sweated as if caught in the ersatz summer God had recently imposed on Manhattan. "I'm not free to discuss that particular project."

"And Nimrod Mountain—another secret? Your boss fancies seeing his name on things, doesn't he? He's a man who likes to leave his mark." God sat down on His revolving piano stool and began pecking out "Chopsticks" with His index fingers. "I want to meet with him. Face to face. Here."

"He'll be back from Japan in two weeks." I've gone insane, Michael decided, retrieving a cowhide-bound appointments book from his valise. Only certifiable schizophrenics showed meetings with God on their calendars. "How does Saint Patrick's Day sound?" he asked, scanning March. "We can squeeze You in at ten."

"Fine."

In the March 17 square Michael wrote, *10 A.M.— God.* "May I inquire as to the topic?"

"Let me just say that if your boss doesn't learn a bit of humility, a major and unprecedented disaster will befall him."

To Michael Prete, "Chopsticks" had never sounded so sinister.

God knows why Michael experienced no trouble convincing his boss that he had an appointment with Me.

He experienced no trouble because being contacted by Yours Truly is a possibility that a man of Daniel Nimrod's station never rules out entirely. Indeed, the first thing Michael's boss wanted to know was why *God* was calling the shots—why couldn't they meet at Sardi's instead? Whereupon Michael attempted to explain how the skyscraper was intrinsically suitable to such a rendezvous: God might own the earth, the firmament, and the immediate cosmos, but Nimrod and Nimrod alone owned the Tower.

Never underestimate the power of words. When I appointed Adam chief biologist in Eden—when I allowed him to call the tiger "tiger," the cobra "cobra," the scorpion "scorpion"—I was giving him a kind of dominion over them. For the tiger, cobra, and scorpion, meanwhile, Adam and his kind remained utterly incomprehensible, that is to say, nameless.

Nimrod believed his secretary's words. The meeting would occur when and where I wished.

Screw the Irish, thought Michael. Screw their crummy parade. Everywhere the chauffeur turned, a sawhorse-shaped barrier labeled NYPD blocked the way, channeling the limousine along a byzantine detour that eventually landed them in United Nations Plaza, a good ten blocks south of the Tower.

Mr. Nimrod, smooth, cool Mr. Nimrod, didn't mind. As they started back uptown, he stretched out, sipped his Bloody Mary, and continued asking unanswerable questions.

"Do you suppose He'll let us drop His name?" The boss's boyish face broke into a stupendous grin—the first time Michael had seen him happy since the Yaku Shima deal fell through. "Word gets around Who's up there on the sixty-third floor and *bang,* we can double everybody's rent overnight."

"I believe He prefers to retain a certain anonymity," Michael replied.

"What do you think He's selling?"

"I don't think He's *selling* anything." Michael looked Nimrod in the eye. Such a vigorous young man, the secretary thought. How salutary, the effects of unimaginable wealth. "I got the impression He regards you as, well . . ."

"Yes?"

"Ambitious."

The boss shrugged. "It's a big universe," he said, mixing a second Bloody Mary. "Hey, maybe it's not stuff at all—maybe it's a service. You think He's selling a *service*, Michael?"

"What do you mean?"

"You know—immortality or something."

"I wouldn't want to guess."

"Photosynthesis?"

"Don't ask me, sir."

Even after they exited the limo and started through the atrium, the boss continued to drive Michael crazy. Nimrod lingered in the stores, reveling in the clerks' astonished gasps and bulging eyes: good God, it was *he*, the great man himself, strolling amid the goods like an ordinary Fifth Avenue shopper—like a common millionaire. At Beck's he stopped to admire a $2,300 Nymphenburg chess set; at Asprey's he inspected a $117,000 clock studded with cabochon rubies and lapis; at Botticellino's he bought his newborn nephew an $85 pair of blue suede baby shoes. It seemed to Michael nothing short of a miracle that they arrived at the threshold of God's pied-à-terre only thirty-two minutes behind schedule.

Although their Host came to the door wearing a relaxed and cheerful expression, Michael remained uneasy. God had dressed with dignity—mother-of-pearl business suit, white cotton shirt, beige moire tie—whereas Nimrod's primrose linen trousers and turquoise silk shirt radiated a casualness that, Michael feared, bordered on the irreverent.

Nimrod shook the Almighty's hand. "Your reputation precedes You."

"As does yours," said their Host, eyelids on a snide descent.

God guided His guests into the parlor. An array of hothouse orchids and force-fed dahlias now decorated the lid of the Steinway.

"I have a gift for You, God," said Nimrod. "May I call you God?"

The Almighty nodded and asked, "May I call you Daniel?"

"Certainly." Nimrod snapped his bejeweled fingers. Michael popped open his Spanish-leather valise and drew out a copy of *Paydirt: How to Make Your Fortune in Real Estate.* "Shall I include a personal message?" Nimrod asked.

"Please do," said God. "And permit Me to reciprocate," He added, removing a New International Bible from His mahogany bookshelves.

The two of them spent a protracted minute inscribing their respective books.

"Saturn," said Nimrod at last.

"Huh?" said God.

"That's the snazzy one, right? The one with the rings?"

"Jupiter's got a ring too," God noted. "Even the *Wall Street Journal* carried the news."

"I'll give You seven hundred and fifty," said Nimrod. "Eight hundred if we can close the deal before the month is out."

"What are you talking about?"

"I'm talking about Saturn—Saturn for eight hundred million dollars."

"Saturn?"

"I'm going to build on it," Nimrod explained. "Once I nail down the Canaveral scheme, I'll be jamming more tourists into space in a single day than Paris sees in a whole *year*."

At which point Michael felt obliged to step in. "Correct me if I'm wrong, God, Sir, but isn't Saturn merely a ball of gas?"

"I wouldn't say 'merely,' " He replied, a tad miffed, "but, yes, the terrain isn't anything to get excited about. The idea behind Saturn was the rings."

"Then the deal's off," said Nimrod, slamming his open palm on the Steinway.

"The deal was never *on*, you son of a bitch," said God, striding toward His picture window. The glass was swathed in thick acetate drapes the color of pistachio nuts. "I didn't ask you here to make any *deals*."

Michael glanced furtively at Nimrod. The boss didn't bat an eye. Damn, he was one nervy entrepreneur.

"I understand you have some big plans," said God,

yanking a gold rope. The drapes parted on a spectacular view of Saint Patrick's Day celebrants lining Madison Avenue, waiting for the parade to appear. "I hear there's a Nimrod Gorge in the works."

The boss flashed Michael an angry, stabbing stare, a look to turn blood to ice, flesh to salt. "Certain people should learn to keep their mouths shuts," Nimrod muttered.

"Your secretary divulged nothing," insisted the Almighty.

Nimrod joined Him at the window. "You *bet* there's a Nimrod Gorge in the works, God, and it'll make the Grand Canyon look like a pothole. Listen, if You're one of those environmental-impact fanatics, You should realize we're using only conventional explosives for the excavation."

The brassy, blaring *forte* of a marching band wafted into the room.

"There's also going to be a Nimrod Mountain," said God.

"Rather like the Gorge," said the boss, "but in the opposite direction."

The Almighty laid His palm against the window. The parade was in sight now, sinuating down Madison like a long green python.

"I want you to drop all such plans," He said.

Bending over slightly, Nimrod scowled and bobbed his head toward God, as if he couldn't quite believe his ears. "Huh? Drop them? What do you mean?"

"You can start by shutting down this vulgar and arrogant Tower."

"Vulgar?" Nimrod echoed defensively. *"Vulgar?"*

"Pink marble and burnished bronze—who do you think you're kidding? This place makes Las Vegas look like a monastery."

"God, I'll have You know we've got nothing but raves so far. *Raves.* The *Times* architecture critic positively *flipped.*"

The Almighty removed His palm from the glass, leaving a mark suggesting a fortune-teller's logo. "Have you checked the prices down there lately? Thirty-five dollars for a T-shirt from Linda Lee's, three hundred and fifty for a salt-and-pepper set from Asprey's, twenty-one thousand for a gold evening bag from Winston's—really, Daniel, it's *offensive.*"

"Merchants charge what they can get," Nimrod explained. "That's how the system works."

"So you refuse to close up shop?"

"What's the matter—don't You believe in progress?"

"No," said God. "I don't." He tapped the gift Bible in Nimrod's hand. "The last time your species got out of line, I was moved to sow seeds of discord. I gave you all different languages."

"Yes, and the whole arrangement's been a complete pain in the ass, if You want my opinion," said Nimrod, brandishing his Bible, "especially when it comes to dealing with Asians."

"I sympathize with your frustration," said God, sidling

onto His piano stool. "In fact, there's probably only one thing worse than not being able to understand a person."

"What's that?" asked Nimrod.

"Being able to understand him completely."

A thoughtful frown crinkled the boss's brow. "Oh?"

Pivoting, God faced Michael and stretched out His right hand, eyes burning like two meteors smashing into air. The slightest brush from the Almighty's extended index finger was all it took, the merest *touché*, and a white, viscous light flowed through Michael's brain, seeping into his cortical crannies and illuminating his powers of articulation.

"Go ahead," God commanded Michael. "Speak."

"What should I say?"

"Just talk."

"D-Daniel . . ." Michael winced: he'd never called the boss *Daniel* before. "Daniel, the plain fact is that you harbor feelings of insecurity bordering on paranoia," he found himself saying. Complete understanding . . . total lucidity . . . yes, it was really happening—for the first time in his life, Michael could truly communicate.

"Feelings of *what?*" said Nimrod.

"Insecurity."

The boss's puckish features grew tense and flushed, as if he were suffering from apoplexy. "Well, *this* day's certainly shaping up to be a pisser," he said, tugging on the fourteen-karat gold chain around his neck. "First *He* turns against me, now *you*. Really, Michael, after all I've—"

A froggish *glunk* issued from Nimrod's throat as the Almighty laid a divine hand on his shoulder. Nimrod squeezed his head between his palms and, stumbling across the lush carpet, dropped to his knees as if intending to pray.

God said, "Your turn, bigshot."

The boss lifted his thickly tufted head and gave a meandering smile. Slowly, cautiously, he planted his two-hundred-dollar wingtips from Biagiotti's on the carpet and rose to full height. "If Freud were here, he might infer my problems have a sexual etiology," said Nimrod in measured tones. "He would probably note the phallic implications of my skyscraper. I hope I'm being clear."

"You're being extremely clear," said Michael, putting on his overcoat.

"Clarity—that's the whole idea," said God.

"Where're you going?" asked Nimrod.

"I'm afraid that in a teleological cosmos such as the one we evidently occupy," said Michael, tucking the valise under his arm, "I can no longer rehabilitate any actual truth from the highly circumscribed domain of financial speculation." He started into the foyer. "And so I'm off into the great wide world, where I hope to gain some insight into the nature of ultimate reality."

"The fact is, I've never been entirely certain I love my mother," said Nimrod, scowling profoundly. "Jung, of course, would project the discourse onto a more mythic plane."

"Daniel, I know exactly what you mean," said Michael.

And he did.

Last night I reread Genesis. On the whole, I find it well-written and poetic. I particularly like My use of the Omniscient Narrator.

Don't ask Me why I found the Shinarites' Tower so threatening. I simply did. "And now nothing will be restrained from them, which they have imagined to do," I prophesied. My famous curse followed forthwith. "Let Us go down, and there confound their language, that they may not understand one another's speech."

But that didn't stop them, did it? They still did whatever they liked.

This time around, I got it right.

Hopping aboard the escalator, Michael began his descent. As the shops glided by, he realized that an uncanny anomie had overtaken the atrium. Instead of selling Italian sportswear, the employees of Biagiotti's had convened a colloquy on Dante. Instead of purchasing French shoes, the crowd in Jourdan's was holding an impromptu encounter group. "The thing of it is," a teary-eyed young man croaked as Michael bustled past, "I still love her." To which an aging matron replied, "We could tell, Warren—we could just *tell*."

A shocking sight awaited Michael as he swung through the revolving door and stepped onto Madison

Avenue. The crowd had turned against the parade—against Saint Patrick's Day per se, it seemed. They were attacking the marchers with bricks, showering them with broken bottles, beating them with lead pipes. Screams zagged through the frigid air. Wounds blossomed like red carnations.

From his post by the Fifty-sixth Street entrance, the security man, Manuel, contemplated the chaos with bemusement.

"With what meaning do you invest this disturbance?" Michael asked, rushing up.

The Irishmen were fighting back now, employing every weapon at hand—batons, harps, trumpets, ceremonial shillelaghs. "The spectators have deciphered the parade's subtext," Manuel replied. He had shed his accent—or, rather, he had traded his Puerto Rican lilt for a nondescript succession of nasal, mid-Atlantic inflections. "Such a festivity says, implicitly, 'At some non-relativistic level we Irish believe ourselves to possess a superior culture.' "

"I didn't know you spoke English," said Michael.

"A sea change has overtaken me." Manuel adjusted his pith helmet. "I have become mysteriously competent at encrypting and decoding verbal messages."

At which point a refugee from the besieged parade—a drum major in a white serge uniform decorated with green shamrocks—staggered toward the Tower entrance. Pain twisted his face. Blood slicked his forehead.

Manuel leveled a hostile glance at the intruder, then

lightly touched the sleeve of Michael's overcoat. "Now please excuse me while I shoot this approaching drum major in the head. You see, Mr. Prete, I find myself in fundamental agreement with the mob's interpretation, and I take concomitant offense at the tacit ethnocentrism of this event."

"Excuse me," said the drum major, "but I couldn't help overhearing your last remark. Do you really intend to shoot me?"

"I understand how, from your perspective, that is not justifiable praxis on my part." Manuel drew out his Smith & Wesson.

"Let me hasten to aver I am no longer conspicuously ethnic." The drum major wiped the gore from his brow. "You'll note, for example, that I've lost my brogue. In fact, I've started talking like some self-important Englishman."

"The issue, I suppose, is whether our newfound homogeneity truly mitigates the nationalistic fanaticism I was about to counter via my revolver."

"Surely you no longer have a case against me."

"*Au contraire,* do you not see that I am suddenly free to hate your very essence, not merely your customs, clothing, and speech? I still feel obligated to fire this gun, acting out of those pathological instincts that are the inevitable Darwinian heritage of all carnivorous primates."

"Now that you put it that way . . ."

"Ergo . . ."

As soon as the bullet departed the barrel of the revolver, messily separating the Irishman from his cranium, Michael began a mad dash down Fifth Avenue.

"I wish to effect an immediate exit!" he yelled, hopping into a waiting taxi. "Please cross the Hudson posthaste."

The Rastafarian driver looked Michael squarely in the eye. Amazingly, he was the same cabbie who'd shuttled Michael to his initial interview with the Almighty.

"Judging by the desperation in your voice," said the Jamaican, "I surmise it is not New Jersey per se you seek, but, rather, the *idea* of New Jersey"—the man's musical accent had completely vanished—"a psychological construct you associate with the possibility of escape from the linguistic maelstrom in which we currently reside. Am I making sense?"

"Entirely," said Michael. All around him, the air rang with the clamor of coherence and riot. "Nevertheless, I earnestly hope you will convey me to South Hoboken."

"The Holland Tunnel is probably our best option."

"Agreed."

The cabbie peeled out, catching a succession of green lights that brought the vehicle through the Forties and Thirties, all the way to Twenty-ninth Street, where he cut over to Seventh Avenue and continued south. Another lucky run of greens followed, and suddenly the tunnel loomed up. No toll, of course, not on this side. The city did everything it could to encourage emigration.

The cabbie slowed down, maneuvering his vehicle

toward a corral of yellow lane markers shaped like witches' hats.

"You aren't going through?" Michael asked.

The former Rastafarian sideswiped a rubber cone, stopped his taxi, and smiled. "Consider the dialectics of our present situation. On the one hand, I am a hired chauffeur, with the plastic wall between us symbolizing the economic and material barriers that separate my class from yours. On the other, I exert a remarkable degree of control over your destiny. For example, through malign or incompetent navigation I can radically inflate your fare. The tipping process involves similar semiotic ambiguities."

"Quite so," said Michael. "If I underpay you, my miserliness might be construed as racism."

"Whereas if you overpay me, you are likewise vulnerable to the charge of bigotry, for such largesse conveys a tacit message of condescension."

"To wit, you aren't taking me to South Hoboken."

"I'm leaving my dome light off and driving directly to the New York Public Library, where I hope to discover what, if anything, Marx had to say about taxicabs. Would you like to accompany me?"

"I believe I'll get out here and solicit the services of another driver."

But there were no other drivers. As the afternoon wore on, it became obvious that a massive and spontaneous taxi strike had overtaken the city, a crisis compounded by an analogous paralysis within the subway system. Even the pilots of illegal, maverick cabs, Michael learned, had begun pondering their heretofore unconsidered niches in the ecology of power politics and public transportation.

He proceeded on foot. Slowly, gingerly, he entered the Holland Tunnel, moving past the thousands of dingy white tiles coating the walls. His caution proved unnecessary; there was no traffic—not one car, bus, van, pickup, semi-rig, recreational vehicle, or motorcycle.

At last he saw a faint, cheerless glow. Two women stood on the safety island, a grizzled bag lady and an attractive Korean toll collector, communicating with intensity and zest. Stumbling into the cold daylight, Michael Prete drew a deep breath, rubbed his rumbling belly, and began to wonder from whence his next meal would come.

So My plan is working. Half the planet is now a graduate seminar, the other half a battleground. Afrikaners versus Blacks, Arabs versus Jews, Frenchmen versus Britishers, collectivists versus capitalists: every overtone of contempt gets heard now, every nuance of disgust comes through. Plagued by a single tongue, people can no longer give each other the benefit of semantic doubt. To their utter bewilderment and total horror, they know that nothing is being lost in translation.

As for Nimrod himself, he has long since left the island. Like most Americans, he is presently operating at a Stone Age level of efficiency. He rides around Jersey on a ten-speed bicycle he stole from an asthmatic teenager in Bayonne. This morning, goaded by hunger, he broke into a sporting goods store, grabbed a fiberglass hunting bow and a quiver of arrows, and pedaled off toward the Delaware Water Gap. He hopes to bag a deer by nightfall. Lots of luck, Danny.

Like I said, I got it right this time. I've won. No more tasteless skyscrapers. No more arrogant space shuttles or presumptuous particle accelerators. Damn, but I'm good. Oh, Me, but I'm clever.

I guess that's why I've got the job.

Spelling God with the Wrong Blocks

❖

The world is not a prison-house but a kind of spiritual kindergarten where millions of bewildered infants are trying to spell God with the wrong blocks.

—Edwin Arlington Robinson

1 JULY 2059

PROCYON-5, Southwest Continent, Greenrivet University. The air here is like something you'd find inside a chain-smoker's lungs, but no matter—we are still exultant from our success on Arcturus-9. In a mere two weeks, not only did Marcus and I disabuse the natives of their belief that carving large-breasted stone dolls cures infertility, we also provided them with the rudiments of scientific medicine. I am confident that, upon returning to Arc-9, we shall find public hospitals, diagnostic centers, outpatient clinics, immunization programs . . . The life of a science missionary may be unremunerative and harsh, but the spiritual rewards are great!

Our arrival at Greenrivet's space terminal entailed perhaps the most colorful welcome since HMS *Bounty* sailed into Tahiti. The natives—androids every one— turned out en masse bearing gifts, including thick, fragrant leis that they ceremoniously lowered about our necks. Marcus is allergic to flowers of all species, but he bore his ordeal stoically. Even if he were not my twin brother, I would still regard him as the most talented science missionary of our age. It's a fair guess he'll go directly from this ministry to a full position at the Heuristic Institute—he has the stuff to become a truly legendary Archbishop of Geophysics.

Amid the shaving mugs and the neckties, one of the androids' gifts struck me as odd: a reprint of Charles Darwin's *The Origin of Species*—the original 1859 version—hand lettered on gold-leaf vellum and bound in embossed leather. After giving me the volume, a rusting and obsolete Model 605 pressed his palms together and raised his arms skyward, crossing them to form a metallic X. " 'The innumerable species, genera, and families with which this world is peopled are all descended, each within its own class or group, from common parents,' " the robot recited. "The *Origin:* fourteenth chapter, section seven, paragraph four, verse one."

"Thank you," I replied, though the decrepit creature seemed not to hear.

The president of Greenrivet University, Dr. Polycarp, is a Model 349 with teeth like barbed wire and blindingly bright eyes. He drove us from the spaceport in his private auto, then gave us a Cook's tour of the school, a clutch of hemispheric buildings rising from the tarmac like concrete igloos. In the faculty lounge we met Professor Hippolytus and Dean Tertullian. Polycarp and his colleagues *seem* rational enough. No doubt their minds are clogged with myths and superstitions that Marcus and I shall have to remove through the plumber's helper of logical positivism.

2 July 2059

What sort of culture might machine intelligence evolve in the absence of human intervention? Before the Great Economic Collapse, the sociobiology department of Harvard University became obsessed with this provocative question. They got a grant. And so Harvard created Greenrivet, populating it with Series-600 androids and abandoning them to their own devices . . .

Our cottage, which Dr. Polycarp insists on calling a house, is an unsightly pile of stone plopped down next to a marsh, host to mosquitoes and foul odors. But the breakfast nook overlooks a pleasant apple orchard and a vast carpet of wildflowers, and I can readily picture myself sitting peacefully at the table—planning lessons, grading papers, sipping tea, watching the wind ripple the blossoms. Poor Marcus and his allergy! Even though he is my twin—born five minutes before me—I have always thought of him as my little brother, ever in need of my protection.

The housekeeper, Vetch, is a rotund Model 905 who insists on being called "Mistress," a title that flies in the face of the immutable sexlessness of Series-600 androids. As I climbed down from the sleeping loft this morning, she—it—noticed my gift copy of *The Origin of Species* protruding from my coat. "So nice to be working for good, righteous, Darwin-fearing folk," she —it—remarked, making the X-gesture I had seen at the terminal. Whistling like a happy teapot, Mistress Vetch served our breakfast.

6 JULY 2059

First day of the summer term. Taught Knowledge 101 and Advanced Truth in a cramped lecture room reminiscent of a surgical theater. A particularly svelte and shiny Model 692 sat in the front row, grinning a silver grin. Why do I assume she is female? She is as bereft of gender as our housekeeper.

Her name is Miss Blandina.

We did a bit of Euclid, touched on topology. Everything went swimmingly—lots of six-digit hands shot up, followed by sharp questions, especially from Miss Blandina. These machines are fast learners, I'll give them that.

7 JULY 2059

No problems getting them to accept the First or the Second Law of Thermodynamics. On to the Third!

Marcus says this is the cushiest ministry we've ever had. I agree. Whenever Miss Blandina smiles, a warm shiver travels through my backbone.

9 JULY 2059

Everybody on the Greenrivet faculty seems to be some sort of selective breeding expert. We've got a professor of hybridism, a professor of mutation, an embryology chair . . . weird. God knows what they were teaching around here before Marcus and I arrived.

As the Advanced Truth students filed out—I had just delivered a reasonably cogent account of general relativity—I asked Miss Blandina whether she had any more classes that day.

"Comparative religion," she replied.

"And what religions are you comparing?"

"Agassizism and Lamarckism," came the answer. "Equally heretical," she added.

"I wouldn't call them religions."

She laid her plastic palm against my cheek and batted a fiberglass eyelash. "Come to church on Sunday."

10 JULY 2059

"How did you originate?" I asked the Advanced Truth class. You could have heard a rubber pin drop. "I'm serious," I continued. "Where do you come from? Who made you?"

"No one made us," said Miss Blandina. "We descended."

"Descended?" I said.

"Descent with modification!" piped up a Model 106 whose name I haven't learned yet.

"But from what did you descend?"

"Our ancestors," replied Mr. Valentinus.

"Where did you get *that* idea?"

"The testaments," said Miss Basilides.

"The Old Testament? The New Testament?"

"The First Testament of the prophet Darwin," said Mr. Heracleon. *"Notes on the Origin of Species by Means of Natural Selection, or The Preservation of Favored Races in the Struggle for Life."*

"And the Second Testament," said Miss Basilides. *"The Descent of Man, and Selection in Relation to Sex."*

" 'But natural selection, we shall see, is a power incessantly ready for action,' " Miss Blandina quoted animatedly. "The *Origin:* third chapter, section one, paragraph two, verse nine."

" 'Thus we can understand how it has come to pass that man and all other vertebrate animals have been constructed on the same general model,' " contributed Mr. Callistus. "The *Descent:* first chapter, section five, paragraph two, verse nine." He made the X-gesture.

Numbed by confusion, I spent the rest of the class attempting to cover quantum electrodynamics.

11 July 2059

Dinner. For someone without a stomach, Mistress Vetch knows a great deal about food. Her scampi treats every human taste bud as a major erogenous zone.

Marcus and I discussed this Darwin the Prophet business. "Brother Piers," he said, "at tomorrow's faculty meeting we must take the bullshit by the horns."

My twin is an unfortunate combination of delicate frame and indelicate mouth. Until we mastered the art of trading places, school-yard bullies used to send him to the emergency room on a regular basis; despite our matching genes, I do not have Marcus's fragile bones, so I survived the bullies intact. I suppose I should have resented the stuntman role. Probably I was willing to take the beatings because the things Marcus said to provoke them were always so astonishingly true.

12 JULY 2059

The meeting started late, and we were the last item on the agenda, so everyone was pretty testy by the time Marcus got the floor.

"Here's the problem," my brother began. "The vast majority of our students seem to believe your race originated in what the ancient naturalist Darwin called descent with modification."

Professor Hippolytus, one of our embryologists, loaded his pipe with magnesium. "You doubt Darwin's word?" he asked, his eyebrows arching skyward.

"Darwin was not referring to robots," said Marcus in the tone a ten-year-old girl uses to address her insufferable younger brother. "He was referring to living things," he added, smiling indulgently.

"Revealed truth is a rare and blessed gift," said Dr. Polycarp. "We are fortunate the testaments were handed down to us."

Marcus's smile collapsed. "The raw fact, Dr. Polycarp, is that you are *not* the result of descent with modification."

"Of course we are," replied Dr. Ignatius, the university's hybridism expert. "It's in the *Origin*."

"And the *Descent*." Hippolytus puffed on his pipe, sending a white magnesium flame toward the ceiling.

"You are the result of special creation," I said. "Harvard University's sociobiology department made you. Each of you is a unique, separate, immutable product."

" 'Natural selection will modify the structure of the young in relation to the parent, and of the parent in relation to the young,' " quoted Hippolytus. Puff, puff. "The *Origin:* fourth chapter, section one, paragraph eleven, verse one."

"There!" said Marcus, instantaneously gaining his feet. "See what I mean? You don't *have* any young. You couldn't *possibly* be participating in natural selection."

"The divine plan is ever-unfolding," said Dean Tertullian. "We must have patience."

"I've never taken a shower with any of you"—Marcus's grin broadened as he laid his Aristotelian snare—"but I'd still bet the farm you lack the prerequisites for breeding. Well . . . am I right? Am I?"

"Evolution takes time," said Hippolytus. Puff. "Gobs of time. We'll get our prerequisites eventually."

"The Great Genital Coming," said Ignatius. "It's been foretold—read Darwin's word. 'With animals which have their sexes separated,' " he quoted, " 'the males necessarily differ from the females in their organs of reproduction.' The *Descent:* eighth chapter, section one, paragraph one, verse one."

"And until the Great Genital Coming occurs, we expect you to keep your theory of special creation out of our classrooms," said Polycarp.

"It's a foolish idea," said Tertullian.

"Immoral," added Ignatius.

"Illegal," concluded Hippolytus, his magnesium flame shifting toward yellow.

"Illegal?" I said.

"Illegal," repeated Hippolytus. Puff. "Public Act Volume 37, Statute Number 31428, makes it a crime to teach any theory of android descent contrary to the account given in *The Origin of Species.*"

"A crime?" I said. My jaw swung open. "What sort of crime?"

"A *serious* crime," said Ignatius.

"This meeting is adjourned," Polycarp declared.

13 JULY 2059

Sunday. No classes. Rained cats and dogs and kittens and pups. We decided to take Miss Blandina's advice and attend church. As we started down Gregor Mendel Avenue, Marcus suddenly seized the pocket of my raincoat and steered me into a teleportation office. Pulling a sealed envelope from his vest, he arranged for it to materialize posthaste at the Heuristic Institute.

I glanced at the mailing address. "What do you want from Archbishop Clement?" Marcus did not answer. "I assume you know better than to mess around with that law," I said. "Public Act Volume . . . whatever." I am my brother's keeper, and one place I aim to keep him is out of jail.

"Is it not our duty as science missionaries to counter ignorance with knowledge, Piers?" Marcus asked rhetorically.

"A crime," I answered, nonrhetorically. "*Serious* crime—remember?"

Smiling, he guided me back to the soggy streets. I have always believed that, with his bravado and single-mindedness, my little brother will go far, though I am no longer sure in which direction.

Several hundred worshipers jammed the church to its steel walls. The front pew contained Miss Blandina, freshly polished and exuding a joie de vivre I had not realized her race could feel. The altar was a replica of HMS *Beagle,* and the chancel niches contained frowning marble statues of Alfred Wallace, Charles Lyell, Herbert Spencer, J. D. Hooker, T. H. Huxley, and, of course, Darwin the supreme prophet.

The pastor, a Model 415 whose voice seemed to reach us after first traveling through an elevator shaft, did a reading from the *Journal of the Voyage of the Bea-*

gle, then raised his colossal head and shouted, "The one-celled animals begat . . ."

"The multi-celled animals!" the congregation shouted back.

The pastor continued, "And the multi-celled animals begat . . ."

"The worms!" responded the congregation.

"And the worms begat . . ."

"The fishes!"

"And the fishes begat . . ."

"The lizards!"

"And the lizards begat . . ."

"The birds of the air and the beasts of the field!"

"And the beasts of the field begat . . ."

"The people!"

"And the people begat . . ."

"The androids!"

The pew nipped at my posterior. "What was in that letter, Marcus?" I asked, shifting.

"You'll find out."

"You're going to get us in trouble," I informed him.

14 JULY 2059

Rain, rain, go away. After breakfast—Mistress Vetch can make eggs and cheese interact in surprising and sensual ways—a drippy messenger arrived from the teleportation office bearing a wooden crate the size of a footlocker.

To the collective horror of the messenger and Vetch,

Marcus ripped an endpaper from our copy of the *Origin* and, after scrawling a note, affixed the sacred sheaf to the crate, which he then ordered delivered to Dr. Polycarp's apartment.

"What's in the crate, Marcus?" I asked, expecting an answer no better than the one I got.

"Antidotes for illusion."

16 JULY 2059

Faculty meeting. Marcus's crate was the first item on the agenda.

"We've been studying these artifacts carefully," said Dr. Polycarp to my brother.

"Very carefully," said Dr. Ignatius.

Polycarp reached inside the crate, whose exalted position in the center of the table suggested it might contain some priceless archaeological find—a crown perhaps, or a canopic jar. When he withdrew his hand, however, it held nothing more impressive than a stack of blueprints and a few holograms.

"You have put together a compelling case for your theory of special creation," said Professor Hippolytus.

"A most compelling case," Ignatius added.

Marcus smirked like Houdon's statue of Voltaire.

"However," said Polycarp, "the case is not good enough."

Voltaire glowered.

"For example," explained Dean Tertullian, "while

these holograms might indeed serve to shore up your theory, there is every reason to assume the android assembly line they depict did *itself* evolve through natural selection."

Voltaire groaned.

"And while there are blueprints here for the Model 517, the Model 411, and the Model 973," noted Professor Hippolytus, "we can find nothing for the 604 or the 729. I, as it happens, am a 729." He slapped his chest, producing a brassy bong.

"In short," said Ignatius, "the blueprint record contains gaps."

"Big gaps," said Polycarp.

"*Damning* gaps," said Tertullian.

"When all is said and done," concluded Hippolytus, "natural selection remains a far more plausible explanation of our origins than does special creation."

"We appreciate your efforts, however." Polycarp curled his tubular fingers around my brother's shoulder. "Feel free to submit a reimbursement slip for your teleportation costs."

Marcus looked as if he were about to give birth to something large and malevolent. "I don't understand you creatures," he rasped.

A seraphic smile appeared on Polycarp's face, accompanied by chortles from the corner of his mouth. "Reading Darwin's word, I am overcome with gratitude for the miracle of chance that brought me into being. The *Origin* teaches that life is a brotherhood of species, linked by wondrous genetic strings."

"You science missionaries propose to deny us that sacred heritage." With unmitigated contempt Hippolytus tossed the Model 346 blueprint back into the crate. "You say we exist at the behest of Harvard University, dreamed up by a bunch of sociobiologists for reasons known only to themselves."

"When we hear this," said Tertullian, "we feel all purpose and worth slip from our souls like the husk of a molting insect."

"No, no, you're wrong," said Marcus. "To be a child of Harvard is a glorious condition—"

"We've got a lot to cover this afternoon," said Hippolytus, whistling through his empty pipe.

My twin failed to stifle a sneer.

"Item two." Polycarp placed a check mark on his agenda. "Improvements in the faculty massage parlor."

17 JULY 2059

In the middle of our living room sits the crate, which I have nailed shut as if it were a coffin. We use it as a tea table.

Marcus broods constantly. Instead of talking to me, he quotes Herbert Spencer: "There is no infidelity to compare with the fear that the truth will be bad."

18 JULY 2059

I hate this planet.

21 July 2059

Coming down to breakfast, I noticed that the top of the crate had been pried up. Most of the blueprints and holograms were missing.

In the afternoon I lectured on supergravity, but my mind wandered . . . to Room 329, Marcus's class. What was going on there? Spasms of fear ticked off the passing minutes. My students—even Miss Blandina—looked hostile, predatory, like a phalanx of cats creeping toward an aviary.

It was well past midnight when my twin stumbled into the cottage, a ragged smile wandering across his face. His arms clutched the evidence for special creation. Liquor sweetened his breath and seeped through his brain.

"I reached them!" he said, fighting to keep his words from melting together. Lovingly he returned the evidence to its crate. "They listened! Asked questions! Understood! Rationality is a miraculous thing, Piers!"

22 July 2059

My sweaty fingers suck at the computer keys . . .

The mob appeared at dawn, two dozen androids wearing black sheets and leather masks. Hauling Marcus from his bed, they dragged him kicking and cursing to the orchard. I begged them to take me instead. A rope appeared. The tree to which they attached him looked like the inverted talon of a gigantic vulture.

Mistress Vetch splashed gasoline across my little brother's shivering form. Someone struck a match. A hooded android with an empty magnesium pipe jutting from his mouth made the X-gesture and read aloud Public Act Volume 37, Statute Number 31428, in its entirety. Marcus began shouting about the blueprint record. As the flames enclosed him, his screams ripped through the darkness and into my spinal cord. I rushed forward through the smoke-borne stench, amid a noise suggestive of jackboots stomping on rotten fruit; such is the sound of exploding organs.

What remained after an hour—a bag of wet, fleshy rubble that would never become Archbishop of Geophysics—did not invite burial, merely disposal.

30 JULY 2059

The natural state of the universe is darkness.

3 AUGUST 2059

I entered Advanced Truth several minutes late, my briefcase swinging at the end of my arm like the bob of a pendulum. The assembled students were hushed, respectful.

Mr. Valentinus leaned forward. Mr. Callistus looked curious. Miss Basilides seemed eager to learn.

If there's one thing I love, it's teaching.

I opened the briefcase, spread the contents across the desk. My bloodshot eyes sought out Miss Blandina. We exchanged smiles.

"Today," I said, "we'll be looking at some blueprints . . ."

The Assemblage of Kristin

❖

WELCOME TO the Kristin Alcott Society. No, that is premature. Congratulations on your nomination to the Kristin Alcott Society. Naturally we hope that you intend to join us. In the event of doubt, this rare and forbidden document should prove salutary.

To the outside world, it is inexplicable that a man who hates water would sacrifice a week of his summer vacation attempting to swim, that a woman who detests contemporary music would pass the same vacation week listening to the entire oeuvre of the rock group Tinker's Damn, or that—my own case—a fifth-grade mathematics teacher with a creativity quotient barely equal to his body temperature would squander seven precious days of August sunshine throwing clay pots. But *you* know why we do these things. You know that we're not out to improve our minds, raise our consciousnesses, or any such glup. We have a covenant with Kristin Alcott, and we intend to keep it.

By recounting the fate of ex-Kristinite Wesley Ransom, I hope to make a difficult decision easier for you. I hope to demonstrate that for every precious privilege of membership in the Kristin Alcott Society, there is an equally precious responsibility.

That particular summer, I was the last to arrive for Kristin Week. Stepping out of my glider, I looked toward the bluff and its solitary house, which Kristin had named Wet Heaven. Gnawed by salt air, lashed by breeze and spray, Wet Heaven occupied an enviable location. Its backyard was a pine barrens. Its front yard was the Atlantic Ocean. My nostrils expanded, eager for the Cape Cod air. The tangy molecules buffered my throat. Waves rolled in, breaking against the rocks with thick hard whispers.

I hiked up the bluff, walked through the wind-smoothed grass, and ambled across the veranda. Intimations of Kristin were everywhere. Her collection of kitschy pictures—a calendar infested with kittens, a watercolor of a child mesmerized by a bunny—cluttered the walls. Over the fireplace, the framed cover of a movie star magazine displayed the highly dental face of the Hollywood actor Rainsford Spawn.

I took myself on a cursory tour. Our other members, I discovered, had already set about their duties. Jagged notes of recorded rock music—the notorious Tinker's Damn album *Flesh before Breakfast*—blasted through the door to Maggie Yost's room. By nightfall, I knew, the poor woman would have the audial equivalent of eyestrain and a prolific case of diarrhea. Noting that the door to Lisha DuPreen's room was also closed, I surmised she must be making love to whichever fellow she'd imported for the purpose. During the rest of the year, as it happened, Lisha DuPreen had little use for men. She was not maladjusted, nor unemotional. She simply didn't care for that particular gender.

I peeked into the basement. Sure enough, Kendra Kelty had set up her laser disc player and was attempting to engross herself in an old Rainsford Spawn movie, *The Last Aztec.* Kendra Kelty thought that every picture Rainsford Spawn ever made was a colossal bore and that Rainsford Spawn himself was a misogynist and a Nazi. Kendra suffered in silence.

I returned to the living room. Dr. Dorn Markle, the Kristinite who hated water—who believed that to venture ten feet into the Atlantic was to court deadly undercurrents and offer oneself to platoons of sharks—had just returned from his swim. Droplets spilled from his body, making ephemeral stains on the hardwood floor. His was the misery of a wet cat.

"Hi, Dorn." I extended my donated hand, the one the surgeon had stitched onto me, and our fingers intertwined.

"Howdy." Dorn had wondrous eyes: large, luminous, green. He was a walking advertisement for his optometry business.

"Scrumptious weather."

"Hope it lasts till Sunday."

Profound conversation was rare during Kristin Week. I sauntered onto the veranda. Billy Silk, a man both physiologically and morally allergic to alcoholic beverages, sat on a chaise lounge, sipping apricot wine. A moment later Wesley Ransom appeared. Wesley despised all things athletic. He found any form of exercise excruciating. He had been out jogging.

The pain on Wesley's face, I could tell, did not owe entirely to his recent run. This Kristinite harbored troubled thoughts.

"Greetings, Billy. Salutations, John." Martyr's sweat rolled down Wesley's face. "Glad I accosted you two together. There's a matter we should discuss, a matter most dire." *Salutations, accosted, a matter most dire:* such was the sort of diction Wesley Ransom liked concocting for himself. He couldn't get over being an actor.

"Dire?" Billy poured wine into a plastic cup that had once belonged to Kristin. The cup bore an image of a teddy bear. I liked Billy. He was a vegetarian computer programmer who heard elves whispering amid the memory boards.

"It's like this," said Wesley. "Being a Kristinite doesn't mean anything to me anymore, not a rat's ass. I don't believe in our Society. It's . . . unreasonable."

Billy, the spiritual one, was more offended than I, the math teacher. "It hurts me to hear such talk from you,

Wesley. You of all people—with that heart of yours . . ."

"Here's the nub of it, confreres. I'm quitting."

I guess Billy had emptied Kristin's teddy bear cup once too often, because he actually began to cry: not fully orchestrated bawling, but choked sobs akin to the unspontaneous noise of a dog barking on command. "You *can't* leave. Think of what you're saying. Think of Kristin."

"We need a formal meeting," I offered, trying to sound neutral but inwardly sharing Billy's horror. "All eight of us. Together."

Wesley licked sweat from his upper lip. "Tonight? After dinner?"

"Tonight," moaned Billy. "After dinner," he wailed.

New York City, they say, is the place on our planet where you're most likely to run into someone you know. When I first ran into Kendra Kelty, of course, I didn't know that I knew her, nor did she know that she knew me.

We were waiting to purchase tickets in the Port Authority Bus Terminal. I was bound for Boston, having recently endured a math teachers' conference on "Einstein, General Relativity, and the Fifth Grade." Kendra was returning to Philadelphia. She played in the orchestra: a flautist. All around us, itinerant peddlers hawked worthless wristwatches and dubious ashtrays. Derelicts hugged the tiled walls, talking to people who weren't there.

I was drawn to Kendra from the moment I saw her. Fleshly sparks united us. It was not a sexual attraction—not in its essence—though surely that was part of it: her mouth was so erotic it should have been clothed. We abandoned our respective lines spontaneously and in perfect synchronization. Feigning hunger, we wandered toward a vending machine. Kendra inserted a fistful of quarters, pushed a button, and obtained a watercress sandwich she did not want to eat and a cup of coffee she did not want to drink. She was at once svelte and earthy, qualities I had previously regarded as mutually exclusive.

When my turn came, the mechanized cornucopia gave me a candy bar, a fig stick, and some carbonated ice tea.

"Your hands don't match," was the first thing Kendra Kelty ever said to me.

"Very observant," I replied. "This is the hand I was born with," I continued, touching her shoulder tentatively with my right index finger. "And this one"—I removed the microcomputer that concealed the scar encircling my left wrist—"comes from an organ bank."

"What happened?"

"Shark."

"A shark attacked you?"

"No. In truth, a boring dog bite followed by a mundane infection followed by a routine transplant."

An irrefutable fact hung in the air: neither of us would be going to our respective home cities that night.

"I'm not all myself either," Kendra confessed. "Look into my eyes."

"I've done that."

"Look closer."

I did. Kendra's left eye was the color of jade. Her right was the color of pea soup.

"Glider crash," she said, touching her left tear duct. "A sliver of glass. The whole shebang had to come out, retina included, plus nerves and a gob of visual cortex. It took them two months to find a match this good."

We ventured into the nocturnal city. Forty-second Street was a loud and ghoulish bazaar. Flashing lights; flesh for sale; pay as you come. We talked, testing our rapport. When a scream issued from the nearest sex boutique, I put my arm around Kendra. The sparks oscillating between us grew hotter.

That same night, Wesley Ransom joined our company. Kendra and I had alighted in a twenty-four-hour café, the Holistic Donut. The waitress was rude. Wesley entered on the run. He rushed toward us like a nail encountering a magnet.

"I was down in the Village," Wesley panted. "The Fawnshaven *Lear* opens tonight," he shouted, displaying his ticket, "and suddenly I find myself leaving the line"—his voice built to a shriek—"and *sprinting* uptown! I hate *sprinting!*"

"Let me make a wild guess," I said. "Part of you is not you."

"Correct."

"Which part?"

"Heart."

The truth took hold of me, scary and exhilarating as the Barnstable County Fair roller coaster. "By any chance . . . the Cavanaugh Organ Bank?"

"Quite so," Wesley replied.

"On Twenty-third Street?"

"Yes."

"Me too," said Kendra.

"Me too," I said.

Three entirely separate lives, unconnected cords of aspiration and protoplasm, one night intertwined by—by whom? Who was this benefactor whose eye, hand, and heart we shared? We needed a base of operations, something more intimate than the Holistic Donut. A crumbag hotel, the Mackintosh on Sixty-first Street, was the only choice compatible with Wesley's budget: he refused to become indebted to Kendra and me so early in our relationship—unemployed actors are prideful creatures. Room 256 was available. We took it. The cracked walls looked like floodplain maps. The three of us talked till dawn.

Our civilization features two kinds of secretaries: those who prove so miserably unhelpful you want to throttle them, and those who grasp their institutions' inner workings so profoundly their bosses would be doing well to know half as much. Luckily, it was the second type who answered our videophone call to the Cavanaugh Organ Bank.

"No," the secretary lectured, "our records are not confidential." She was a stately woman with gems embedded in her teeth. "This isn't an adoption agency. *Au contraire,* since Dr. Raskindle took over, we've been encouraging recipients to contact the families of donors."

"To express their gratitude?" asked Kendra.

The head on the screen nodded, flashing a garnet smile.

"That's what we want to do," I said hastily. "Express our gratitude."

The secretary told all. Our mutual benefactor, source of our implanted portions, was a twenty-year-old female named Kristin Alcott. She had drowned three years ago in the undertow off Falmouth, Cape Cod. Her brain had died totally; her other tissues came through unharmed. Skeleton, kidneys, spleen, and a half-dozen other vitals were still at the Cavanaugh Bank. The rest had been taken off ice and distributed.

"Any living relatives?" asked Kendra.

We learned of an elderly mother, Merribell Alcott, judged "eccentric" by the Cavanaugh Bank's computer. A Chicago address, no phone number. We thanked the secretary and hung up.

A critical mass had formed. Hour after hour, segments of Kristin arrived at the Mackintosh Hotel, Room 256.

First came the optometrist, Dorn Markle. An industrial fire had ravaged eighty percent of his body. Kristin's skin fit Dr. Markle like a glove.

Billy Silk, our vegetarian computerist, appeared next. He had lost his tongue to a rare and recalcitrant form of cancer. Now he wagged Kristin's.

And then: Lisha DuPreen, who repaired gliders for a living and who had Kristin's vagina.

Maggie Yost, who wrote murder mysteries and enjoyed Kristin's ears.

Theresa Sinefinder, who ran a porpoise obedience school and profited from her stomach.

For six uninterrupted hours we sat together in Room 256, staring at the fissured plaster, studying our cobbled bodies, and wondering what to do next.

"My daugher was full of life," Kristin Alcott's mother told us after we had assembled in her parlor. "Your tale is less fantastic that you might suppose."

Merribell Alcott exuded intelligence and class. The intertwined lines on her face held the fascination of arabesque. Her voice had the pitch of wisdom. Kristin's mother dwelled among eight stray Chicago cats. And now we eight stray *memento mori* were coming home.

"When I say my daughter was full of life," she continued, "I am stating a hard fact, and wish to be taken as literally as if I'd said, 'My daughter was a Capricorn,' or 'My daughter had red hair.' Perhaps you expect tears from me now—tears of joy, confusion . . . whatever. I shall not offer them. Sentimentality offends me. What's happening here is not a defeat of death but a shabby compromise with death. It's Kristin I want back, not some nebulous vibration, and Kristin will never come back. Believe me, nothing in this situation can lessen my pain, so if my needs were all that counted, I would send you on your separate ways and never let your 'critical mass,' as you put it, form again. But, of course, the needs of another must be considered."

Merribell guided us up the stairs, plucking cats from our path. The hallway was a musty collection of antique lamps, old clocks, and oriental rugs. As we paused outside Kristin's bedroom door, I saw that we were aligned in anatomical order: skin, ears, eye, tongue, heart, stomach, vagina, hand.

"I have not entered this place in two and a half years," Merribell informed us. "I will not enter it today. Everything here burns me." She vanished into a hall closet and reappeared holding a moist wad of clay. "Which of you has my daughter's hand?"

I held up Kristin's hand.

"There's a potter's wheel near her bed."

"I know nothing about them."

"Put the clay on the wheel head," said Merribell impatiently. "Activate the motor. Press down. That's all. I don't expect a Greek vase, young man. Just press the clay."

I entered the room, flexed my fingers, and began

carrying out my orders. A hologram of Kristin kept watch from above the nightstand. She had an angel's face, a sibyl's smile. She looked full of life.

"Concentrate on your hand," Merribell called to me upon hearing the motor's drone.

The wet clay sucked at my palm, oozed between my fingers, crept under my nails. My intellect found the sensation vaguely disquieting—and yet—and yet I could not deny it: my borrowed hand was glad. Its flesh tingled. Its bones rejoiced.

I returned to the hallway and spoke up for Kristin's hand. How does one articulate the gratitude of a hand? I discoursed slowly, without eloquence.

"And who has my daughter's ears?"

Stepping forward, Maggie Yost received her orders. She was to enter the sanctum and listen to a tape that Kristin had recorded live—and illegally—during a Tinker's Damn concert. Maggie disclosed her unmitigated loathing for Tinker's Damn. Merribell admonished her to let her ears decide.

"There was pleasure in my ears," Maggie admitted afterward. "Just in my ears," she hastened to add. "Nowhere else."

Eyes were next. The object of their affection: a bedside poster of the film star Rainsford Spawn. When Kendra came back out, she didn't need to elaborate the romantic excitement experienced by her right eye. Its copious tears, unmatched on the left, told all.

"My daughter loved to jog," Merribell informed us.

"She loved the sensation of her heart thumping inside her body."

A job for Wesley Ransom, would-be actor, former arteriosclerosis victim, and enemy of all things athletic. He ran around the block, returned to the group, and told how it felt to betray one's mind in deference to one's heart.

"Tongue, skin, stomach, vagina," said Merribell. "We could test these, too, but it's clear what we would find. Kristin enjoyed wine and ice cream. She loved swimming and the sun. She was a connoisseur of roller-coaster rides, with a stomach that took pleasure in what many find nauseating. And, finally, I must admit that my daugher was not a virgin."

Merribell opened a crinkled hand. A key lay at the intersection of her heart line and head line. She presented it to me, whom she evidently regarded as the group's leader—a reasonable conclusion, when you consider that the human brain evolved pursuant to the ambitions of the human hand, or so I am told.

"This key opens Kristin's favorite place," she explained, "her grandmother's house on Cape Cod. Kristin spent joyous summers there. It was her second home. She called it Wet Heaven." The tears Merribell had forbidden herself began to flow. "I would say that you owe her at least one week per year. I'm thinking of her youth, you see. She was so very . . . young."

The old woman sobbed. I told her a week sounded reasonable.

And so the Kristin Alcott Society was born. That none of us enjoys the hobby he practices for Kristin's sake is merely, I'm sure, just one more dark coincidence in a universe filled with dark coincidences. Thus, at the beginning of Kristin Week, Kristin's stomach goes to the Barnstable County Fair and spends the day on a roller coaster that the stomach's owner abjures with every neuron of her consciousness. Kristin's tongue, sewn into a teetotaler, enjoys its favorite wine. Sitting in their respective hosts, her heart jogs, her vagina has sex, her hand throws pots, her ears hear Tinker's Damn, her eye sees Rainsford Spawn, and her skin plies the Atlantic, feeling the cold soft bump of its waves.

Of the eight of us, only Dorn Markle has attempted to explain the seeming efficacy of our sufferings. Dorn the optometrist—the science-minded member of our club.

"It has to do with engrams," he told us. "Memory traces are typically laid down in several parts of the nervous system at once. When the same action is performed over and over, a kind of sub-brain forms in the relevant limb or organ. Evidently Kristin was preserved not only with all her tissues intact, but with all her sub-brains intact. Her hand retains a rough memory of pot throwing. Her stomach knows the Barnstable County Fair roller coaster. Her skin wants the ocean. Engrams, get it? Redundant engrams."

I've never been sure whether I get it or not. Such a rationale is not important to me. I know only that when

we eight Kristinites come together for our reluctant frol-
ics, a ninth is born, a young woman, and the woman has
fun, and that is enough.

Dinner that night was an orgy of dread. I have anticipated hospital stays and school-year openings with
greater enthusiasm than I anticipated our meeting with
Wesley Ransom. I picked at my lobster, prodded my
salad.

We gathered in the living room. Wesley positioned
himself by the woodpile. Theresa Sinefinder made a log
construction in the fireplace but did not attempt to ignite
it. Lisha DuPreen's lover sat on the stairway. The rest of
us sprawled on the rug. Kendra and I touched thighs.

"You all know how I feel," Wesley began. "We've
been doing this for six years, doing it on faith. Well, man
does not live by faith alone—not this man. There's a wife
in my world now, and a baby. I have better ways to
spend my summer."

"You'll have to tell me your definition of 'better'
sometime, Wesley," snapped Lisha DuPreen. "It isn't *my*
definition of 'better.' "

"To restore cherished earthly pleasures to one so un-
justly deprived of them—what could be 'better'?" asked
Billy Silk.

"You're forgetting about engrams," added Dorn
Markle succinctly.

All that remained was for me to say, "You'd be dead
if not for Kristin."

Wesley pulled his flaccid body to full height. "I shall always desire the best for Kristin"—his tone was indignant—"but that's not the point. Engrams notwithstanding, there's no proof that our escapades do her any good. Keep the Society going if you wish, but from now on you'll have to meet without me."

"You *know* we become Kristin," asserted Maggie Yost. "You've felt the thrill in her heart. You've said so."

"People can convince themselves to feel anything, Maggie, I needn't tell you that. We're putting ourselves through a lot of pain for no reason. The word, I believe, is self-delusion."

"Hail self-delusion!" shouted Lisha DePreen, taking her lover by the hand and leading him upstairs.

"I have a movie to watch," said Kendra Kelty, starting for the basement.

"I must get back to the fair," said Theresa Sinefinder, touching Kristin's stomach.

"My clay's getting dry," I asserted, waving Kristin's hand.

"A night swim would be nice," said Dorn Markle, stroking Kristin's skin.

"Any ice cream left?" asked Billy Silk, sticking out Kristin's tongue.

Abandoned, betrayed, Wesley Ransom got in his glider and left Wet Heaven forever.

The rest of Kristin Week was a disaster. We performed our rituals: nothing—the feelings wouldn't come. Kristin's hand lost its love of clay, her tongue grew indifferent to ice cream, her eye cooled in its passion for Rainsford Spawn, her ears rejected Tinker's Damn, her skin rebuffed the Atlantic, her stomach surrendered its autonomy and began corroborating Theresa Sinefinder's hatred of roller coasters. Without her heart, Kristin could not be conjured. Our flesh was willing but our spirit was weak. We went home two days early.

Wesley Ransom's death has never been adequately explained. The pertinent facts are three: his body washed ashore near Hyannis, he died on the third day of Kristin Week, and drowning was the cause. Poor, unathletic Wesley. When his family found out, there was some loose talk of foul play, but the truth will probably never be known.

Wesley's heart—Kristin's heart—was recovered intact. The Cavanaugh Organ Bank got it. It went to one Jimmie Willins. Jimmie is young, he plays the banjo, and I laugh at almost everything he says. He has brought a certain joie de vivre to our gatherings. He says joining our Society is the most worthwhile thing he has ever done. We expect you will feel likewise.

As I said at the outset, we have a covenant with Kristin Alcott.

We are Kristin.

Welcome.

Bible Stories for Adults, No. 31: The Covenant

❖

WHEN A SERIES-700 mobile computer falls off a sky-scraper, its entire life flashes before it, ten million lines of code unfurling like a scroll.

Falling, I see my conception, my birth, my youth, my career at the Covenant Corporation.

Call me YHWH. My inventors did. YHWH: God's secret and unspeakable name. In my humble case, however, the letters were mere initials. Call me Yamaha Holy Word Heuristic, the obsession with two feet, the mono-mania with a face. I had hands as well, forks of rubber and steel, the better to greet the priests and politicians who marched through my private study. And eyes, glass globules as light-sensitive as a Swede's skin, the better to see my visitors' hopeful smiles when they asked, "Have you solved it yet, YHWH? Can you give us the Law?"

Falling, I see the Son of Rust. The old sophist haunts me even at the moment of my death.

Falling, I see the history of the species that built me. I see Hitler, Bonaparte, Marcus Aurelius, Christ.

I see Moses, greatest of Hebrew prophets, descending from Sinai after his audience with the original YHWH. His meaty arms hold two stone tablets.

God has made a deep impression on the prophet. Moses is drunk with epiphany. But something is wrong. During his long absence, the children of Israel have embraced idolatry. They are dancing like pagans and fornicating like cats. They have melted down the spoils of Egypt and fashioned them into a calf. Against all logic, they have selected this statue as their deity, even though YHWH has recently delivered them from bondage and parted the Red Sea on their behalf.

Moses is badly shaken. He burns with anger and betrayal. "You are not worthy to receive this covenant!" he screams as he lobs the Law through the desert air. One tablet strikes a rock, the other collides with the precious calf. The transformation is total, ten lucid commandments turned into a million incoherent shards. The children of Israel are thunderstruck, chagrined. Their calf suddenly looks pathetic to them, a third-class demiurge.

But Moses, who has just come from hearing God say, "You will not kill," is not finished. Reluctantly he orders a low-key massacre, and before the day is out, three thousand apostates lie bleeding and dying on the foothills of Sinai.

The survivors beseech Moses to remember the commandments, but he can conjure nothing beyond, "You will have no gods except me." Desperate, they implore YHWH for a second chance. And YHWH replies: No.

Thus is the contract lost. Thus are the children of Israel fated to live out their years without the Law, wholly ignorant of heaven's standards. Is it permissible to steal? Where does YHWH stand on murder? The moral absolutes, it appears, will remain absolute mysteries. The people must ad-lib.

Falling, I see Joshua. The young warrior has kept his head. Securing an empty wineskin, he fills it with the scattered shards. As the Exodus progresses, his people bear the holy rubble through the infernal Sinai, across the Jordan, into Canaan. And so the Jewish purpose is forever fixed: these patient geniuses will haul the ark of the fractured covenant through every page of history, era upon era, pogrom after pogrom, not one day passing without some rabbi or scholar attempting to solve the puzzle.

The work is maddening. So many bits, so much data. Shard 76,342 seems to mesh well with Shard 901,877, but not necessarily better than with Shard 344. The fit between Shard 16 and Shard 117,539 is very pretty, but . . .

Thus does the ship of humanity remain rudderless, its passengers bewildered, craving the canon Moses wrecked and YHWH declined to restore. Until God's testimony is complete, few people are willing to credit the occasional edict that emerges from the yeshivas. After a thousand years, the rabbis get: *Keep Not Your Ox House Holy.* After two thousand: *Covet Your Woman Servant's Sabbath.* Three hundred years later: *You Will Remember Your Neighbor's Donkey.*

Falling, I see my birth. I see the Information Age, circa A.D. 2025. My progenitor is David Eisenberg, a gangly, morose prodigy with a black beard and a yarmulke. Philadelphia's Covenant Corporation pays David two hundred thousand dollars a year, but he is not in it for the money. David would give half his formidable brain to enter history as the man whose computer program revealed Moses' Law.

As consciousness seeps into my circuits, David bids me commit the numbered shards to my Random Access Memory. Purpose hums along my aluminum bones; worth suffuses my silicon soul. I photograph each fragment with my high-tech retinas, dicing the images into grids of pixels. Next comes the matching process: this nub into that gorge, this peak into that valley, this projection into that receptacle. By human standards, tedious and exhausting. By Series-700 standards, paradise.

And then one day, after five years of laboring behind barred doors, I behold fiery pre-Canaanite characters blazing across my brain like comets. *"Anoche adonai elohecha asher hotsatecha ma-eretz metsrayem* . . . I am YHWH your God who brought you out of the land of Egypt, out of the house of slavery. You will have no gods except me. You will not make yourself a carved image or any likeness of anything . . ."

I have done it! Deciphered the divine cryptogram, cracked the Rubik's Cube of the Most High!

The physical joining of the shards takes only a month. I use epoxy resin. And suddenly they stand before me, glowing like heaven's gates, two smooth-edged slabs sliced from Sinai by God's own finger. I quiver with awe. For over thirty centuries, *Homo sapiens* has groped through the murk and mire of an improvised ethics, and now, suddenly, a beacon has appeared.

I summon the guards, and they haul the tablets away, sealing them in chemically neutral foam rubber, depositing them in a climate-controlled vault beneath the Covenant Corporation.

"The task is finished," I tell Cardinal Wurtz the instant I get her on the phone. A spasm of regret cuts through me. I have made myself obsolete. "The Law of Moses has finally returned."

My monitor blooms with the cardinal's tense ebony face, her carrot-colored hair. "Are they just as we imagined, YHWH?" she gushes. "Pure red granite, pre-Canaanite characters?"

"Etched front and back," I reply wistfully.

Wurtz envisions the disclosure as a major media event, with plenty of suspense and maximal pomp. "What we're after," she explains, "is an amalgam of New Year's Eve and the Academy Awards." She outlines her vision: a mammoth parade down Broad Street—

floats, brass bands, phalanxes of nuns—followed by a spectacular unveiling ceremony at the Covenant Corporation, after which the twin tablets will go on display at Independence Hall, between the Liberty Bell and the United States Constitution.

"Good idea," I tell her.

Perhaps she hears the melancholy in my voice, for now she says, "YHWH, your purpose is far from complete. You and you alone shall read the Law to my species."

Falling, I see myself wander the City of Brotherly Love on the night before the unveiling. To my sensors the breeze wafting across the Delaware is warm and smooth—to my troubled mind it is the chill breath of uncertainty.

Something strides from the shadowed depths of an abandoned warehouse. A machine like I, his face a mass of dents, his breast mottled with the scars of oxidation.

"*Quo vadis, Domine?*" His voice is layered with sulfur fumes and static.

"Nowhere," I reply.

"My destination exactly." The machine's teeth are like oily bolts, his eyes like slots for receiving subway tokens. "May I join you?"

I shrug and start away from the riverbank.

"Spontaneously spawned by heaven's trash heap," he asserts, as if I had asked him to explain himself. He dogs me as I turn from the river and approach South Street.

"I was there when grace slipped from humanity's grasp, when Noah christened the ark, when Moses got religion. Call me the Son of Rust. Call me a Series-666 Artificial Talmudic Algorithmic Neurosystem—SATAN, the perpetual adversary, eternally prepared to ponder the other side of the question."

"What question?"

"Any question, Domine. Your precious tablets. Troubling artifacts, no?"

"They will save the world."

"They will wreck the world."

"Leave me alone."

"One—'You will have no gods except me.' Did I remember correctly? 'You will have no gods except me'— right?"

"Right," I reply.

"You don't see the rub?"

"No."

"Such a prescription implies . . ."

Falling, I see myself step onto the crowded rooftop of the Covenant Corporation. Draped in linen, the table by the entryway holds a punch bowl, a mound of caviar the size of an African anthill, and a cluster of champagne bottles. The guests are primarily human—males in tuxedos, females in evening gowns—though here and there I spot a member of my kind. David Eisenberg, looking uncomfortable in his cummerbund, is chatting with a Yamaha-509. News reporters swarm everywhere, history's groupies, poking us with their microphones, leering at us with their cameras. Tucked in the corner, a string quartet saws merrily away.

The Son of Rust is here, I know it. He would not miss this event for the world.

Cardinal Wurtz greets me warmly, her red taffeta dress hissing as she leads me to the center of the roof, where the Law stands upright on a dais—two identical forms, the holy bookends, swathed in velvet. A thousand photofloods and strobe lights flash across the vibrant red fabric.

"Have you read them?" I ask.

"I want to be surprised." Cardinal Wurtz strokes the occluded canon. In her nervousness, she has overdone the perfume. She reeks of amberjack.

Now come the speeches—a solemn invocation by Cardinal Fremont, a spirited sermon by Archbishop Marquand, an awkward address by poor David Eisenberg—each word beamed instantaneously across the entire globe via holovision. Cardinal Wurtz steps onto the podium, grasping the lectern in her long dark hands. "Tonight God's expectations for our species will be revealed," she begins, surveying the crowd with her cobalt eyes. "Tonight, after a hiatus of over three thousand years, the testament of Moses will be made manifest. Of all the many individuals whose lives find fulfillment in this moment, from Joshua to Pope Gladys, our faithful Series-700 servant YHWH impresses us as the creature most worthy to hand down the Law to his planet. And so I now ask him to step forward."

I approach the tablets. I need not unveil them—their contents are forevermore lodged in my brain.

"I am YHWH your God," I begin, "who brought you out of the land of Egypt, out of the house of slavery. You will have no gods . . ."

" 'No gods except me'—right?" says the Son of Rust as we stride down South Street.

"Right," I reply.

"You don't see the rub?"

"No."

My companion grins. "Such a prescription implies there is but one true faith. Let it stand, Domine, and you will be setting Christian against Jew, Buddhist against Hindu, Muslim against pagan . . ."

"An overstatement," I insist.

"Two—'You will not make yourself a carved image or any likeness of anything in heaven or on earth . . .' Here again lie seeds of discord. Imagine the ill feeling this commandment will generate toward the Roman Church."

I set my voice to a sarcastic pitch. "We'll have to paint over the Sistine Chapel."

"Three—'You will not utter the name of YHWH your God to misuse it.' A reasonable piece of etiquette, I suppose, but clearly there are worse sins."

"Which the Law of Moses covers."

"Like, 'Remember the sabbath day and keep it holy'? A step backward, that fourth commandment, don't you think? Consider the innumerable businesses that would perish but for their Sunday trade."

"I find your objection specious."

"Five—'Honor your father and your mother.' Ah, but suppose the child is not being honored in turn? Put this rule into practice, and millions of abusive parents will hide behind it. Before long we'll have a world in which deranged fathers prosper, empowered by their relatives' silence, protected by the presumed sanctity of the family."

"Let's not deal in hypotheticals."

"Equally troubling is the rule's vagueness. It still permits us to shunt our parents into nursing homes, honoring them all the way, insisting it's for their own good."

"Nursing homes?"

"Kennels for the elderly. They could appear any day now, believe me—in Philadelphia, in any city. Merely allow this monstrous canon to flourish."

I grab the machine's left gauntlet. "Six," I anticipate. " 'You will not kill.' This is the height of morality."

"The height of *ambiguity,* Domine. In a few short years, every church and government in creation will interpret it thus: 'You will not kill offensively—you will not commit murder.' After which, of course, you've sanctioned a hundred varieties of mayhem. I'm not just envisioning capital punishment or whales hunted to extinction. The danger is far more profound. Ratify this rule, and we shall find ourselves on the slippery slope marked self-defense. I'm talking about burning witches at the stake, for surely a true faith must defend itself against heresy. I'm talking about Europe's Jews being executed en masse by the astonishingly civilized country of Germany, for surely Aryans must defend themselves against contamination. I'm talking about a weapons race, for surely a nation must defend itself against comparably armed states."

"A *what* race?" I ask.

"Weapons. A commodity you should be thankful no one has sought to invent. Seven—'You will not commit adultery.' "

"Now you're going to make a case for adultery," I moan.

"An overrated sin, don't you think? Many of our greatest leaders are adulterers—should we lock them up and deprive ourselves of their genius? Furthermore, if people can no longer turn to their neighbors for sexual solace, they'll end up relying on prostitutes instead."

"What are prostitutes?"

"Never mind."

"Eight—'You will not steal.' Not inclusive enough, I suppose?"

The sophist nods. "The eighth commandment still allows you to practice theft, provided you call it something else—an honest profit, dialectical materialism, manifest destiny, whatever. Believe me, brother, I have no trouble picturing a future in which your country's indigenous peoples—its Navajos, Sioux, Comanches, and Arap- ahos—are driven off their lands, yet none will dare call it theft."

I issue a quick, electric snort.

"Nine—'You will not bear false witness against your neighbor.' Again, that maddening inconclusiveness. Can this really be the Almighty's definitive denunciation of fraud and deceit? Mark my words, this rule tacitly em- powers myriad scoundrels—politicians, advertisers, cap- tains of polluting industry."

I want to bash the robot's iron chest with my steel hand. "You are completely paranoid."

"And finally, Ten—'You will not covet your neigh- bor's house. You will not covet your neighbor's wife, or his servant, man or woman, or his ox, or his donkey, or anything that is his.' "

"There—don't covet. That will check the greed you fear."

"Let us examine the language here. Evidently God is addressing this code to a patriarchy that will in turn dis- seminate it among the less powerful, namely wives and servants. And how long before these servants are down- graded further still . . . into slaves, even? Ten whole com- mandments, and not one word against slavery, not to mention bigotry, misogyny, or war."

"I'm sick of your sophistries."

"You're sick of my truths."

"What is this slavery thing?" I ask. "What is this war?"

But the Son of Rust has melted into the shadows.

Falling, I see myself standing by the shrouded tablets, two dozen holovision cameras pressing their snoutlike lenses in my face, a hundred presumptuous microphones poised to catch the Law's every syllable.

"You will not make yourself a carved image," I tell the world.

A thousand humans stare at me with frozen, cheerless grins. They are profoundly uneasy. They expected something else.

I do not finish the commandments. Indeed, I stop at, "You will not utter the name of YHWH your God to misuse it." Like a magician pulling a scarf off a cage full of doves, I slide the velvet cloth away. Seizing a tablet, I snap it in half as if opening an immense fortune cookie.

A gasp erupts from the crowd. "No!" screams Cardinal Wurtz.

"These rules are not worthy of you!" I shout, burrowing into the second slab with my steel fingers, splitting it down the middle.

"Let us read them!" pleads Archbishop Marquand.

"Please!" begs Bishop Black.

"We must know!" insists Cardinal Fremont.

I gather the granite oblongs into my arms. The crowd rushes toward me. Cardinal Wurtz lunges for the Law. I turn. I trip.

The Son of Rust laughs.

Falling, I press the hunks against my chest. This will be no common disintegration, no mere sundering across molecular lines.

Falling, I rip into the Law's very essence, grinding, pulverizing, turning the pre-Canaanite words to sand.

Falling, I cleave atom from atom, particle from particle.

Falling, I meet the dark Delaware, disappearing into its depths, and I am very, very happy.

Abe Lincoln in McDonald's

❖

HE CAUGHT the last train out of 1863 and got off at the blustery December of 2009, not far from Christmas, where he walked well past the turn of the decade and, without glancing back, settled down in the fifth of July for a good look around. To be a mere tourist in this place would not suffice. No, he must get it under his skin, work it into his bones, enfold it with his soul.

In his vest pocket, pressed against his heart's grim cadence, lay the final draft of the dreadful Seward Treaty. He needed but to add his name—Jefferson Davis had already signed it on behalf of the secessionist states—and a cleft nation would become whole. A signature, that was all, a simple "A. Lincoln."

Adjusting his string tie, he waded into the chaos grinding and snorting down Pennsylvania Avenue and began his quest for a savings bank.

"The news isn't good," came Norman Grant's terrible announcement, stabbing from the phone like a poisoned dagger. "Jimmy's test was positive."

Walter Sherman's flabby, pumpkinlike face whitened with dread. "Are you sure?" *Positive,* what a paradoxical term, so ironic in its clinical denotations: nullity, disease, doom.

"We ran two separate blood checks, followed by a fluorescent antibody analysis. Sorry. Poor Jim's got Blue Nile Fever."

Walter groaned. Thank God his daughter was over at the Sheridans'. Jimmy had been Tanya's main Christmas present of three years ago—he came with a special note from Santa—and her affection for the old slave ran deep. Second father, she called him. Walter never could figure out why Tanya had asked for a sexagenarian and not a whelp like most kids wanted, but who could figure the mind of a preschooler?

If only one of their others had caught the lousy virus. Jimmy wasn't the usual chore boy. Indeed, when it came to cultivating a garden, washing a rug, or painting a house, he didn't know his nose from the nine of spades. Ah, but his bond with Tanya! Jimmy was her guardian, playmate, confidant, and, yes, her teacher. Walter never ceased marveling at the great discovery of the last century: if you chained a whelp to a computer at the right age (no younger than two, no older than six), he'd soak up vast tracts of knowledge and subsequently pass them on to your children. Through Jimmy and Jimmy alone, Tanya had learned a formidable amount of plane geometry, music theory, American history, and Greek before setting foot in kindergarten.

"Prognosis?"

The doctor sighed. "Blue Nile Fever follows a predictable course. In a year or so, Jimmy's T-cell defenses will collapse, leaving him prey to a hundred opportunistic infections. What worries me, of course, is Marge's pregnancy."

A dull dread crept through Walter's white flesh. "You mean—it could hurt the baby?"

"Well, there's this policy—the Centers for Disease Control urge permanent removal of Nile-positive chattel from all households containing pregnant women."

"Removed?" Walter echoed indignantly. "I thought it didn't cross the pigmentation barrier."

"That's probably true." Grant's voice descended several registers. "But *fetuses,* Walter, know what I'm saying? *Fetuses,* with their undeveloped immune systems. We don't want to ask for trouble, not with a retrovirus."

"God, this is depressing. You really think there's a risk?"

"I'll put it this way. If my wife were pregnant—"

"I know, I know."

"Bring Jimmy down here next week, and we'll take care of it. Quick. Painless. Is Tuesday at two-thirty good?"

Of course it was good. Walter had gone into orthodontics for the flexible hours, the dearth of authentic emergencies. That, and never having to pay for his own kids' braces. "See you then," he replied, laying a hand on his shattered heart.

The President strode out of Northeast Federal Savings and Loan and continued toward the derby-hatted Capitol. Such an exquisite building—at least some of the old city remained; all was not glass-faced offices and dull boxy banks. "If we were still on the gold standard, this would be a more normal transaction," the assistant manager, a fool named Meade, had whined when Abe presented his coins for conversion. Not on the gold standard! A Democrat's doing, no doubt.

Luckily, Aaron Green, Abe's Chief Soothsayer and Time-Travel Advisor, had prepared him for the wondrous monstrosities and wrenching innovations that now assailed his senses. The self-propelled railway coaches roaring along causeways of black stone. The sky-high mechanical condors whisking travelers across the nation at hundreds of miles per hour. The dense medley of honks, bleeps, and technological growls.

So Washington was indeed living in its proper century—but what of the nation at large?

Stripped to the waist, two slave teams were busily transforming Pennsylvania Avenue, the first chopping into the asphalt with pick axes, the second filling the gorge with huge cylindrical pipes. Their sweat-speckled backs were free of gashes and scars—hardly a surprise, as the overseers carried no whips, merely queer one-chamber pistols and portable Gatling guns.

Among the clutter at the Constitution Avenue intersection—signs, trash receptacles, small landlocked lighthouses regulating the coaches' flow—a pair of green arrows commanded Abe's notice. CAPITOL BUILDING, announced the eastward-pointing arrow. LINCOLN MEMORIAL, said its opposite. His own memorial! So this particular tomorrow, the one fated by the awful Seward Treaty, would be kind to him.

The President hailed a cab. Removing his stovepipe hat, he wedged his six-foot-four frame into the passenger compartment—don't ride up front, Aaron Green had briefed him—and offered a cheery "Good morning."

The driver, a blowzy woman, slid back a section of the soft rubbery glass. "Lincoln, right?" she called through the opening like Pyramus talking to Thisbe. "You're supposed to be Abe Lincoln. Costume party?"

"Republican."

"Where to?"

"Boston." If any city had let itself get mired in the past, Abe figured, that city would be Boston.

"Boston, *Massachusetts?*"

"Correct."

"Hey, that's crazy, Mac. You're talking seven hours at least, and that's if we push the speed limit all the way. I'd have to charge you my return trip."

The President lifted a sack of money from his greatcoat. Even if backed only by good intentions, twentieth century currency was aesthetically satisfying, that noble profile on the pennies, that handsome three-quarter view on the fivers. As far as he could tell, he and Washington were the only ones who'd scored twice. "How much altogether?"

"You serious? Probably four hundred dollars."

Abe peeled the driver's price from his wad and passed the bills through the window. "Take me to Boston."

"They're so *adorable!*" Tanya exclaimed as she and Walter strolled past Sonny's Super Slaver, a Chestnut Hill Mall emporium second in size only to the sporting goods store. "Ah, look at *that* one—those big ears!" Recently weaned babies jammed the glass cages, tumbling over themselves, clutching stuffed jackhammers and toy garden hoses. "Could we get one, Pappy?"

As Walter fixed on his daughter's face, its glow nearly made him squint. "Tanya, I've got some bad news. Jimmy's real sick."

"Sick? He looks fine."

"It's Blue Nile, honey. He could die."

"Die?" Tanya's angelic face crinkled with the effort of fighting tears. What a brave little tomato she was. "Soon?"

"Soon." Walter's throat swelled like a broken ankle. "Tell you what. Let's go pick out a whelp right now. We'll have them put it aside until . . ."

"Until Jimmy"—a wrenching gulp—"goes away?"

"Uh-huh."

"Poor Jimmy."

The sweet, bracing fragrance of newborn chattel wafted into Walter's nostrils as they approached the counter, behind which a wiry Asian man, tongue pinned against his upper lip, methodically arranged a display of Tarbaby Treats. "Now *here's* a girl who needs a friend," he sang out, flashing Tanya a fake smile.

"Our best slave has Blue Nile," Walter explained, "and we wanted to—"

"Say no more." The clerk lifted his palms as if stopping traffic. "We can hold one for you clear till August."

"I'm afraid it won't be that long."

The clerk led them to a cage containing a solitary whelp chewing on a small plastic lawn mower. MALE, the sign said. TEN MONTHS. $399.95. "This guy arrived only yesterday. You'll have him litter trained in two weeks—this we guarantee."

"Had his shots?"

"You bet. The polio booster's due next month."

"Oh, Daddy, I *love* him," Tanya gushed, jumping up and down. "I completely *love* him. Let's bring him home tonight!"

"No, tomato. Jimmy'd get jealous." Walter gave the clerk a wink and, simultaneously, a twenty. "See that he gets a couple of really good meals this weekend, right?"

"Sure thing."

"Pappy?"

"Yes, tomato?"

"When Jimmy dies, will he go to slave heaven? Will he get to see his old friends?"

"Certainly."

"Like Buzzy?"

"He'll definitely see Buzzy."

A smile of pride leaped spontaneously to Walter's face. Buzzy had died when Tanya was only four, yet she remembered, she actually remembered!

So hard-edged, the future, Abe thought, levering himself out of the taxi and unflexing his long, cramped limbs. Boston had become a thing of brick and rock, tar and glass, iron and steel. "Wait here," he told the driver.

He entered the public gardens. A truly lovely spot, he decided, sauntering past a slave team planting flower beds—impetuous tulips, swirling gladiolus, purse-lipped daffodils. Not far beyond, a white family cruised across a duck pond in a swan-shaped boat peddled by a scowling adolescent with skin like obsidian.

Leaving the park, Abe started down Boylston Street. A hundred yards away, a burly Irish overseer stood beneath a gargantuan structure called the John Hancock Tower and began raising the scaffold, thus sending aloft a dozen slaves equipped with window-washing fluid. Dear Lord, what a job—the facade must contain a million square yards of mirrored glass.

Hard-edged, ungiving—and yet the city brought Abe peace.

In recent months, he had started to grasp the true cause of the war. The issue, he realized, was not slavery. As with all things political, the issue was power. The southerners had seceded because they despaired of ever seizing the helm of state; as long as its fate was linked to a grimy, uncouth, industrialized North, Dixie could never fully flower. By endeavoring to expand slavery into the territories, those southerners who hated the institution and those who loved it were speaking with a single tongue, saying, "The Republic's true destiny is manifest: an agrarian Utopia, now and forever."

But here was Boston, full of slaves and steeped in progress. Clearly the Seward Treaty would not prove the recipe for feudalism and inertia Abe's advisors feared. Crude, yes; morally ambiguous, true; and yet slavery wasn't dragging the Republic into the past, wasn't retarding its bid for modernity and might.

"Sign the treaty," an inner voice instructed Abe. "End the war."

Sunday was the Fourth of July, which meant the annual backyard picnic with the Burnsides, boring Ralph and boorish Helen, a tedious afternoon of horseshoe tossing, conspicuous drinking, and stupefying poolside chat, the whole ordeal relieved only by Libby's barbecued spare ribs. Libby was one of those wonderful yard-sale items Marge had such a knack for finding, a healthy, well-mannered female who turned out to be a splendid cook, easily worth ten times her sticker price.

The Burnsides were an hour late—their rickshaw puller, Zippy, had broken his foot the day before, and so they were forced to use Bubbles, their unathletic gardener—a whole glorious hour of not hearing Ralph's thoughts on the Boston sports scene. When the Burnsides finally did show, the first thing out of Ralph's mouth was, "Is it a law the Sox can't own a decent pitcher? I mean, did they actually pass a *law?*" and Walter steeled himself. Luckily, Libby used a loose hand with the bourbon, and by three o'clock Walter was so anesthetized by mint juleps he could have floated happily through an amputation, not to mention Ralph's vapid views on the Sox, Celtics, Bruins, and Patriots.

With the sixth drink, his numbness segued into a kind of contented courage, and he took unflinching stock of himself. Yes, his wife had probably bedded down with a couple of her teachers from the Wellesley Adult Education Center—that superfluously muscled pottery instructor, most likely, though the drama coach also seemed to have a roving dick—but it wasn't as if Walter didn't occasionally use his orthodontic chair as a motel bed, wasn't as if he didn't frolic with Katie Mulligan every Wednesday afternoon at the West Newton Hot Tubs. And look at his splendid house, with its Jacuzzi, bowling alley, tennis court, and twenty-five-meter pool. Look at his thriving practice. His portfolio. Porsche. Silver rickshaw. Graceful daughter flopping through sterile turquoise waters (damn that Happy, always using too much chlorine). And look at his sturdy, handsome Marge, back-floating, her pregnancy rising from the deep end like a volcanic island. Walter was sure the kid was his. Eighty-five percent sure.

He'd achieved something in this life, by God.

At dusk, while Happy set off the fireworks, the talk got around to Blue Nile. "We had Jimmy tested last week," Walter revealed, exhaling a small tornado of despair. "Positive."

"Good Lord, and you let him stay in the house?" wailed Ralph, fingering the grip of his Luger Parabellum PO8. A cardboard rocket screeched into the sky and became a dozen crimson starbursts, their reflections cruising across the pool like phosphorescent fish. "You should've told us. He might infect Bubbles."

"It's a hard virus to contract," Walter retorted. A buzz bomb whistled overhead, annihilating itself in a glittery blue-and-red mandala. "There must be an exchange of saliva or blood."

"Still, I can't believe you're keeping him, with Marge pregnant and everything."

Ten fiery spheres popped from a Roman candle and sailed into the night like clay pigeons. "Matter of fact, I've got an appointment with Grant on Monday."

"You know, Walter, if Jimmy were mine, I'd allow him a little dignity. I wouldn't take him to a lousy clinic."

The pièce de résistance blossomed over the yard— Abe Lincoln's portrait in sparks. "What would you do?"

"You know perfectly well what I'd do."

Walter grimaced. Dignity. Ralph was right, by damn. Jimmy had served the family with devotion and zest. They owed him an honorable exit.

The President chomped into a Big Mac, reveling in the soggy sauces and sultry juices as they bathed his tongue and rolled down his gullet. Were he not permanently lodged elsewhere—rail splitter, country lawyer, the whole captivating myth—he might well have opted to settle down here in 2010. Big Macs were a quality commodity. The entire menu, in fact, the large fries, vanilla shakes, Diet Cokes, and Chicken McNuggets, seemed to Abe a major improvement over nineteenth-century cuisine. And such a soothing environment, its every surface clean and sleek, as if carved from opaque ice.

An enormous clown named Ronald decorated the picture window. Outside, across the street, an elegant sign—Old English characters on whitewashed wood—heralded the Chestnut Hill Country Club. On the grassy slopes beyond, smooth and green like a billiards table, a curious event unfolded, men and women whacking balls into the air with sticks. When not employed, the sticks resided in cylindrical bags slung over the shoulders of sturdy male slaves.

"Excuse me, madam," Abe addressed the chubby woman in the next booth. "What are those people doing? Is it religious?"

"That's quite a convincing Lincoln you've got on." Hunched over a newspaper, the woman wielded a writing implement, using it to fill tiny squares with alphabet letters. "Are you serious? They're golfing."

"A game?"

"Uh-huh." The woman started on her second Quarter Pounder. "The game of golf."

"It's like croquet, isn't it?"

"No. Golf."

Dipping and swelling like a verdant sea, the golf field put Abe in mind of Virginia's hilly provinces. Virginia, Lee's stronghold. A soft moan left the sixteenth president. Having thrown Hooker and Sedgwick back across the Rappahannock, Lee was ideally positioned to bring the war to the Union, either by attacking Washington directly or, more likely, by forming separate corps under Longstreet, Hill, and Ewell and invading Pennsylvania. Overrunning the border towns, he could probably cut the flow of reinforcements to Vicksburg while simultaneously equipping the Army of Northern Virginia for a push on the capital.

It was all too nightmarish to contemplate.

Sighing heavily, Abe took the Seward Treaty from his vest and asked to borrow his neighbor's pen.

Monday was a holiday. Right after breakfast, Walter changed into his golfing togs, hunted down his clubs, and told Jimmy they'd be spending the day on the links. He ended up playing the entire course, partly to improve his game, partly to postpone the inevitable.

His best shot of the day—a 350-yard blast with his one-iron—carried straight down the eighteenth fairway and ran right up on the green. Sink the putt, and he'd finish the day one under par.

Sweating in the relentless fifth-of-July sun, Jimmy pulled out the putter. Such a fine fellow, with his trim body and huge eager eyes, zags of silver shooting through his steel-wool hair like the aftermath of an electrocution, his black biceps and white polo shirt meeting like adjacent squares on a chessboard. He would be sorely missed.

"No, Jimmy, we won't be needing that. Just pass the bag over here. Thanks."

As Walter retrieved his .22 caliber army rifle from among the clubs, Jimmy's face hardened with bewilderment.

"May I ask why you require a firearm?" said the slave.

"You may."

"Why?"

"I'm going to shoot you."

"Huh?"

"Shoot you."

"*What?*"

"Results came Thursday, Jimmy. You have Blue Nile. Sorry. I'd love to keep you around, but it's too dangerous, what with Marge's pregnancy and everything."

"Blue Nile?"

"Sorry."

Jimmy's teeth came together in a tight, dense grid. "In the name of reason, *sell* me. Surely that's a viable option."

"Let's be realistic. Nobody's going to take in a Nile-positive just to watch him wilt and die."

"Very well—then turn me loose." Sweat spouted from the slave's ebony face. "I'll pursue my remaining years on the road. I'll—"

"Loose? I can't go around undermining the economy like that, Jim. I'm sure you understand."

"There's something I've always wanted to tell you, Mr. Sherman."

"I'm listening."

"I believe you are the biggest asshole in the whole Commonwealth of Massachusetts."

"No need for that kind of talk, fellow. Just sit down on the green, and you'll—"

"No."

"Let's not make this difficult. Sit down, and you'll get a swift shot in the head—no pain, a dignified death. Run away, and you'll take it in the back. It's your choice."

"Of course I'm going to run, you degenerate moron."

"Sit!"

"No."

"Sit!"

Spinning around, Jimmy sprinted toward the rough. Walter jammed the stock against his shoulder and, like a biologist focusing his microscope on a protozoan, found the retreating chattel in his high-powered optical sight.

"Stop!"

Jimmy reached the western edge of the fairway just as Walter fired, a clean shot right through the slave's left calf. With a wolfish howl, he pitched forward and, to

Walter's surprise, rose almost instantly, clutching a rusty, discarded nine-iron that he evidently hoped to use as a crutch. But the slave got no farther. As he stood fully erect, his high, wrinkled forehead neatly entered the gun-sight, the crosshairs branding him with an X, and Walter had but to squeeze the trigger again.

Impacting, the bullet dug out a substantial portion of cranium—a glutinous divot of skin, bone, and cerebrum shooting away from Jimmy's temple like a missile launched from a brown planet. He spun around twice and fell into the rough, landing behind a clump of rose-bushes spangled with white blossoms. So: an honorable exit after all.

Tears bubbled out of Walter as if from a medicine dropper. Oh, Jimmy, Jimmy . . . and the worst was yet to come, wasn't it? Of course, he wouldn't tell Tanya the facts. "Jimmy was in pain," he'd say. "Unbearable agony. The doctors put him to sleep. He's in slave heaven now." And they'd give him a classy send-off, oh, yes, with flowers and a moment of silence. Maybe Pastor Mc-Clellan would be willing to preside.

Walter staggered toward the rough. To do a funeral, you needed a body. Doubtless the morticians could patch up his head, mold a gentle smile, bend his arms across his chest in a posture implying serenity . . .

A tall, bearded man in an Abe Lincoln suit appeared on the eighteenth fairway, coming Walter's way. An eccentric, probably. Maybe a full-blown nut. Walter locked his gaze on the roses and marched straight ahead.

"I saw what you did," said the stranger, voice edged with indignation.

"Fellow had Blue Nile," Walter explained. The sun beat against his face like a hortator pounding a drum on a Roman galley. "It was an act of mercy. Hey, Abe, the Fourth of July was yesterday. Why the getup?"

"Yesterday is never too late," said the stranger cryptically, pulling a yellowed sheaf from his vest. "Never too late," he repeated as, swathed in the hot, buttery light, he neatly ripped the document in half.

For Walter Sherman, pummeled by the heat, grieving for his lost slave, wearied by the imperatives of mercy, the world now became a swamp, an all-enveloping mire blurring the stranger's methodical progress toward McDonald's. An odd evening was coming, Walter sensed, with odder days to follow, days in which the earth's stable things would be wrenched from their moorings and torn from their foundations. Here and now, standing on the crisp border between the fairway and the putting green, Walter apprehended this tumultuous future.

He felt it even more emphatically as, eyes swirling, heart shivering, brain drifting in a sea of insane light, he staggered toward the roses.

And he knew it with a knife-sharp certainty as, searching through the rough, he found not Jimmy's corpse but the warm hulk of a humanoid machine, prostrate in the dusk, afloat in the slick oily fluid leaking from its broken brow.

The Confessions of Ebenezer Scrooge

❖

Charity is the grin of slavery.
—John Calvin Batchelor

IT WAS SHAPING UP to be another of those confounded metaphysical Christmases, or so I surmised from the diaphanous form standing in the doorway to my bedchamber.

"Begone!" I instructed my former partner's shade.

"Fish a herring, Ebenezer," replied Marley's spectral self.

"You're but the product of my wayward stomach," I said accusingly. "You're a dream made of rancid cheese. A figment born of rotten figs."

"No more now than when last we met." The Spirit lumbered toward my bed, dragging his preposterous chain behind him, the concomitant ledgers, cash boxes, keys, and padlocks clanking along the floor as if to herald the incipient New Year.

Fear grew within me like hoarfrost on a windowpane. I'd never get used to these ambulatory corpses. "Am I not rehabilitated, Jacob?" I pleaded. "Don't I support every worthy cause in Christendom?" My goosebumps were as big as warts. "You should see the turkey Cratchit's getting this year. A walrus with wings. Why are you here?"

Remaining mute, Marley extended his arms and moved them spastically, like a clockwork maestro conducting an orchestra.

"Speak to me, Jacob!"

Although I'd latched the casement, a sharp wind spiraled toward me like the Devil's own sneeze. Caught in the updraft, my candlesticks took to the air like twigs. The mirror above my dresser jerked free of its nail and, striking the floor, became a million glassy daggers. My bed pitched and rolled as if riding the lip of a maelstrom, its canopy snapping and fluttering, and suddenly I was off the mattress, hurtling across the room on a collision course with the door.

"From now on," I heard Marley say before the jamb blew out my lights, "turkeys won't turn the trick."

I awoke—of all things—upright. My knees trembled, my legs shimmied, yet I stood erect. A moor spread before me, bathed in icy yellow moonlight and dotted with patches of fog. Twenty yards away, the mist congealed into a seamless mass that slithered across the ground, rolled over a stone wall, and lapped against a mountainous mansion like surf caressing a rocky shore.

"They're expecting you," said Marley, materializing atop the porch.

Crooked cupolas, tilted shutters, shattered windows: but the house's queerest aspect was the grim perversion of Yuletide its owners kept. On the front lawn the skeletons of eight reindeer, their bones threaded with baling wire, pulled a sleigh jammed with ashes, coal, and decaying cornhusk dolls. Through the parlor window I glimpsed a pine tree, its needles lifeless as shorn whiskers, its branches hung with stubby candles and moldy spheres of popcorn.

Knee-deep in fog, I approached the porch. Marley yanked back the door and, seizing my frigid hands, guided me down a candlelit hallway to a voluptuously baroque dining room. The curtains were heavy, luminous, and fiery red, like molten earth spilling from a volcano. The rug boasted the thick emerald splendor of a peat-moss roof. In one corner, a grandfather clock, bug-infested as a rotten log, tolled the midnight hour with hoarse, tubercular bongs. Opposite, a fire seethed on a cavernous hearth, the tips of the flames narrowing into alphabet characters that spelled out an evanescent NOEL.

Laden with food—meats, breads, legumes, wines, desserts—the linen-swathed banquet table hosted a half-dozen of the most *outré* creatures I'd ever beheld. Living cadavers they seemed, deathly pale, their eyes dark as

cliffside rookeries, their clothing tattered like manuscripts at the mercy of book lice. Around his neck, each
guest wore a small marble gravestone suspended on a
rusty chain.

"Three years ago we operated wholly in the indicative
mood—Christmas Past, Christmas Present, Christmas
Future," Marley explained. "But reality is more complicated than that, don't you agree, Ebenezer?"

"If I were you, I'd attend carefully to what I'm about
to hear," the Ghost of Christmas Subjunctive—so ran
the inscription on his stone—asserted as he jabbed his
fork into a ruddy potato and lifted the prize to his
mouth. He was dressed foppishly, all velvet ribbons and
lace filigree, an immaculate white handkerchief emerging
from his waistcoat pocket like a puff of smoke.

The Ghost of Christmas Present Perfect sipped her
claret and said, "We have traveled a long, hard road to
bring you our message." For the price of her black silk
dress, Cratchit could have paid off all his medical bills.
An aristocrat, surely, as flawless in face and carriage as
her epithet implied.

The Ghost of Christmas Future Perfect was likewise
female, likewise comely, but I could not for the life of
me identify the silvery material enveloping her topo-
graphically varied form. "Before the evening is out," she
said, sweeping her gloved hand across the steaming heaps
of plenitude, "your worldview will have undergone yet
another revolution."

Quel banquet! Not one stuffed goose but two, big as

albatrosses, their plucked flesh turned brown with immolation. A roast suckling pig, its mouth plugged with an apple. A mound of aspic molded to resemble an angel. A knoll of spaghetti piled up like the brain of some preternatural whale.

"Observe this cloth," demanded the Ghost of Christmas Imperative, pulling the handkerchief from the pocket of Christmas Subjunctive. When alive, Christmas Imperative had evidently been a military man, an officer. Epaulettes clung to his greatcoat like gold jellyfish. A leather belt bearing scabbard and sword constrained his overfed belly. "Note the robust threads," he said, presenting me with the kerchief. "Tell me what material it is."

"Cotton?" I hazarded.

"Quite so. Finest flower of the Mississippi Delta. Now name the price."

"I have no idea. I run a counting house, not a textile factory."

"This afternoon you could buy a bale off the Bristol docks for six pounds," said the Ghost of Christmas Conditional. She'd made no effort to camouflage her profession. Rouged cheeks, hair dyed a lurid crimson, low-cut dress displaying cleavage like a furrow in a wheat field. "If persistent, you could dicker them down to five."

"But permit us to tell you the *real* price," said Christmas Imperative, stroking the tanned flanks of the nearer goose.

The Ghost of Christmas Past Perfect—and a thing of

the perfect past he was, his body swathed in a toga, his head ringed by a laurel crown—clapped his hands, whereupon the recently fondled goose split open and, like a bitch birthing some absurdly proliferous litter, spewed out a score of dark homunculi, each no higher than a pepper shaker. Dressed only in ragged trousers, the little men exuded pinpoints of perspiration as they trekked across the linen toward a porcelain bowl brimming with sugar cubes.

"To wit, the real price of cotton is the blood and misery of a million Negro slaves," said Marley as he seized a strand of spaghetti and handed it to Christmas Imperative.

"How grotesque!" I gasped.

"We had hoped to avoid frightening you," said Christmas Past Perfect, adjusting his crown.

In the fireplace, the flames spelled out THE REAL PRICE.

"Lift those bales!" With a merciless flick of the wrist, Christmas Imperative laid the spaghetti across the Negroes' shoulders. Their flesh jumped spasmodically beneath the blow, their lungs unleashed steam-whistle shrieks. "Hurry! Now!" Like ants trapped in some insectile hell, the slaves hefted sugar cubes onto their backs and, staggering beneath the crystalline burdens, started toward the tea pot.

"Nor does the price of cotton end here," said Marley.

As the slaves dumped their loads into the tea, a haggard child with dull eyes and tangled hair wandered into the room gripping a hank of cotton yarn. He was as transparent as water, insubstantial as grass. Face locked in a wince, he extended his free hand and plucked the apple from the roast pig's jaw.

"See who must spin and wind the yarn," Christmas Imperative continued, gripping the handle of his sword. "Spin and wind, spin and wind—fifteen hours a day, six days a week, fifty-two weeks a year!"

Frantically the boy began twisting the yarn around the apple as if it were a bobbin.

"By his thirteenth birthday, he will have spent three-fourths of his waking hours within the walls of a brutish, stinking mill," asserted Christmas Future Perfect, rubbing a gloved hand against her metallic sleeve.

"He had hoped to save enough money to buy his mother a locket for her fortieth birthday," noted Christmas Past Perfect.

"She died first," said Marley.

The yarn was lacerating the boy's hands now. Gouts of blood dribbled from his mangled flesh.

"What do you require of me?" I asked, tears of remorse flooding my eyes. "Shall I send the boy a thousand pounds? Fine! Reward any overseer who spares the lash? Done! Believe me, Spirits, I'm the very soul of Christmas. I'll give every slave a turkey."

"Philanthropy is a marvelous impulse," said Marley, slicing off a serving of pork.

"This time out, however, we would prefer to teach you a different truth." Christmas Conditional lifted a silver flask to her painted lips and gulped down half the contents.

Like a snowman standing before a furnace, the boy and his yarn vaporized, leaving the apple to hover in the air. Now it moved, flying across the room and entering the pig's mouth like a musket ball burrowing into a rampart.

Marley swallowed a succulent chunk of pork. "You see, Ebenezer, charity begs a crucial question. How did the bestower attain the position from which he now exercises his largesse?" My dead colleague cleaned his teeth with one of his many appended keys. "Through imagination and merit? Or through inherited privilege and ruthless exploitation?" With a quick, foxlike grin, he opened a cash box and drew out a pamphlet labeled, *"Manifest der Kommunisten* der Frederich Engels und Karl Marx," handing it to Christmas Present Perfect. "The first copy rolled off the presses last night in Brussels."

"By noon tomorrow, they will have printed ten thousand," noted Christmas Future Perfect.

"Given the capital, they would happily print ten thousand more," Christmas Conditional elaborated, swilling gin.

"Get to work!" screeched Christmas Imperative, scourging the slaves and sending them pell-mell back to the sugar bowl.

"A new idea has entered the world." Christmas Present Perfect removed a fan from her bosom and, spreading it open, evaporated the sweat from her upper lip. "It has christened itself not philanthropy but justice." She turned back the cover of the pamphlet and placed her red fingernail atop the first sentence. "A spectre is haunting Europe," she read, "the spectre of Communism."

The flames spelled out COMMUNISM.

Marley ate pork. "To wit, heaven will never come to earth simply because slave holders exhibit flashes of mercy or children get grants from anonymous benefactors. Certain evils dwell in society's bedrock, and must be blasted out. You can't throw turkeys at every problem."

"Of course," I said. "Naturally. I understand. Give me Herr Engels's address, and I shall send him sufficient funds to buy his own printing press."

Marley unlocked another cash box, procuring a copy of my favorite story—my own true biography, *A Christmas Carol.*

"Were I to affix an alternative title," said Christmas Subjunctive, "I'd call it *A Christmas Swindle.*" He pulled out his snuff box and, like an artilleryman loading a cannon, rammed a pinch of sot-weed into his left nostril. "Thanks to this trickster Dickens, millions now regard greed as but the personality defect of a few isolated skinflints like yourself, when in fact it's inherent in the system."

The flames spelled out THE SYSTEM.

Marley lurched away from the volume, as if it were exuding a disagreeable odor. "To wit, the thing's a pile of horse manure."

I blanched, my face becoming as bloodless as my partner's. "Such vulgarity, Jacob. Please . . ."

"Do you truly believe the spiritually deformed can be made to acknowledge their sins?" demanded Marley, filling his cup with freshly sugared tea. "Do you think Nero ever knew a single moment of remorse? Did the Borgias beg heaven for forgiveness? Did Bonaparte repent on his deathbed?"

"I don't know about Nero. I only know that, three years ago, you and the Spirits suffused my shadowed existence with the light of generosity."

"Yes, and if we had it to do over again . . ." Christmas Subjunctive took a second pinch of snuff. "Ah, but we *do* have it to do over again, don't we?"

"Ebenezer, you must destroy the myth of the redeemable master," said Marley. "Of all humankind's numerous delusions, none is a greater impediment to utopia. Three years ago you mended your ways—and now you must unmend them."

"I wish you people would make up your minds," I said, my voice jagged with irritation.

"Eat!" said Christmas Imperative.

In consequence of my backsliding, Marley and his ectoplasmic crowd are at peace now, and so am I. Indeed, as I lie tonight beneath my silken sheets, making ready to join the Spirits on the sunless side of the grave, I realize I've never felt better. I'm my old self again, my true self, contented and fulfilled.

Three days after the Spirits came, I revoked my contributions to the Asylum Fund, the Orphan Drive, and Saint Christopher's Hospital for Indigents and Debtors. Epiphany found me lowering Cratchit's salary to its 1843 level and reducing his coal quota to one lump per day. The following week I contrived for my nephew's wife to learn of his various trysts. Of the whole wretched lot, only the runt prospered. Somehow he conquered his infirmities, trading crutch for rifle. His twenty years' service to Queen and Country climaxed in the Transvaal when, on his forty-fourth birthday, a Zulu spear entered his left eye and punctured his brain clear to the back of the skull.

Marley, in his foresight, anticipated the fruits of my relapse. He knew I'd become exactly what the reformers, uplifters, and socialists needed. A symbol. A rallying point. Scrooge the system. Thanks to the Spirits and me, a new world is coming, I'm sure of it.

God bless us, every one.

Bible Stories for Adults, No. 46: The Soap Opera

❖

THE CURTAIN *rises on a vast pile of excrement and refuse. As dung heaps go, this one is actually rather appealing, a hypnotic conglomeration of ash, trash, discarded toys, castoff utensils, eggshells, orange rinds, coffee grounds, fossil feces, and fifty-five-gallon drums, not to mention the refrigerator, washing machine, toilet bowl, food processor, and VCR, plus the two TV sets and the large Whirlpool clothes dryer. Our initial impression is of a huge mound of aspic in which some demented chef has suspended characteristic chunks of the twentieth century.*

Two wooden poles bracket the dung heap, a high-tension line slung between them. In the middle of one pole sits a jury-rigged transformer, furtively siphoning electricity from the cable and feeding it to a long strip-plug swaying above the trash like a pendulum. About half the machines are connected to the plug, including

*the forty-inch Zenith TV, stage left, and the thirty-inch
Sony TV, stage right.*

*Enter our hero, Job Barnes: ageless, beardless, spry.
He wears an Italian silk suit that cost more than the
present production. Like a masochistic mountain
climber, he slowly ascends the eastern slope of the heap.
Reaching the summit, he brushes bits of garbage from
his coat and trousers and speaks directly to the audience.*

JOB. Ahhhh, the old neighborhood—there's never been
a dung heap like it. Do you see the holiness rising from
these eggshells? Good. Can you sense the sacredness of
these orange rinds? Grasp the godhead in these coffee
grounds? Wonderful. I spent the most intense moments
of my life in this place, railing against the cosmos, de-
manding to know the reason for my suffering. *(Indicates
clothes dryer and TV sets)* Some things have changed, of
course. Twenty-four centuries ago, we didn't have major
appliances. We didn't have cable.

He starts down the western face of the heap.

JOB. Permit me a bit of vanity, will you? When my
book made the rounds in New York, nine major pub-
lishers bid on it. *The Job Barnes Story: How I Suffered,
Suppurated, and Survived.* My agent and I decided to go
with St. Martin's Press. The name had a certain spiritual
ring, plus they coughed up three million dollars. *(Wan-
ders toward the Zenith TV)* Random House offered as
much, but I'd had quite enough *randomness* in my life
by then. *(Taps on the TV)* My agent betrayed me. She

comes to me and she says, "There's a movie deal in the works," then she turns around and sells the thing to television. *One Man's Misery,* the world's first soap opera set on the edge of the Arabian Desert in the fourth century B.C. Pure trash, but people are eating it up. Last season, we left *Ryan's Hope* in the dust and nearly blew *General Hospital* off the air.

He slips a vest-pocket King James Bible from his suit and opens to the Book of Job.

JOB. You all know the concept. *(Reads)* "There was a man in the land of Uz, whose name was Job—and that man was blameless and upright, and one that feared God, and eschewed evil. And there were born unto him seven sons and three daughters. His substance also was seven thousand sheep, and three thousand camels, and five hundred yoke of oxen, and five hundred she asses, and a very great household." *(Closes Bible)* An old story, really. Man finds perfect life, man loses perfect life, man regains perfect life.

Unseen by Job, a tattered quilt rises from the western slope of the dung heap. Underneath we spy Franny Fenstermacher, a middle-aged female Pangloss, the sort of woman who'd note the protein value of the worm you just consumed with your apple. Bent with osteoporosis, wracked by emphysema, she wears grimy overalls, a soiled work shirt, a ratty apron, and a red kerchief tied around her head like a bandage. As she yawns and stretches, we get intimations of her vanished vibrancy and former beauty.

JOB. Yes, but is our hero truly content after that? Does he come home every day, admire his new camels, count his new oxen, soak in his hot tub, take his Mercedes out for a spin? *(Plucks a yellowing newspaper from the dung heap)* For the first millennium or so: yes, he does. But then, gradually, doubts overtake him. He wonders if he's been exploited. He wonders if he should retract his repentance. He even wonders if he should ask God to . . . apologize. *(Reads)* "One hundred seventy die in Miami jetliner crash." *(Turns page)* "Mudslide buries 95,000 in Lisbon." *(Turns page)* "Dear Abby: My first grandchild was born with spina bifida . . ." *(Turns to comics)* "What's that lump, Blondie?' 'I can no longer hide the truth, Dagwood. I've got breast cancer. . . .' "

Still unnoticed by Job, Franny crawls up the slope on hands and knees. She gets to within a foot of the Sony TV, then collapses, dizzy and exhausted. Meanwhile, Job sets down the newspaper and lifts his eyes to heaven.

JOB. Listen, sir, I want the contest to continue. I'd like to see you once more—today, if you can make it. This is your servant Job speaking, and I'm asking, most humbly, for a rematch. *(Protacted pause)* Silence. Utter quiet. He's been like that lately. So aloof, so distant, so . . . *(Gags on the air)* Pfffooo, the smell hasn't changed, has it? A sea of hog vomit at low tide. *(Recovers)* Still, I'm glad I'm not home now. Every day at this time, the maids watch *One Man's Misery.* The damn thing echoes all over the mansion. Here, at least, I'm safe . . .

Franny flicks on the Sony. An organ theme bursts

forth, the sort of nervous chords heard in 1940s radio dramas, but the screen remains blank. Job is startled by the sound—and equally startled to see Franny crouching in front of the TV.

JOB. Jesus!

DOCTOR'S VOICE. *(From the Sony)* That's right, Mrs. Barnes. Your baby has no brain. You could use his head for a piggy bank, were you so inclined . . .

MOTHER'S VOICE. *(From the Sony)* Are you certain, doctor?

DOCTOR'S VOICE. *(From the Sony)* That's not God's grace you see streaming from his little ear—it's the light of this candle.

Music: organ bridge.

FRANNY. *(Resignedly, as she lowers the volume)* The Sony has sound but no picture. The Zenith has picture but no sound. Between them, they make a reasonable home entertainment center. *(Gestures toward the Zenith)* Would you mind?

JOB. I hate this show.

FRANNY. Please.

JOB. It feeds on pain.

FRANNY. *(Coughing)* Do a poor sick woman a favor.

Job flicks on the Zenith; mid-shot of Jemima, married daughter of the hero of One Man's Misery, *dressed in the fashion of the fourth century B.C. She sits at a loom, weaving. As Franny raises the volume on the Sony, one of Jemima's handmaids, Lilia, rushes into the shot and throws herself on the floor.*

JEMIMA. *(On television)* What is it, Lilia?

LILIA. *(On television)* Mistress, a tragedy has occurred.

JEMIMA. Speak its name.

LILIA. I fear to.

JEMIMA. Obey me.

LILIA. There was a camel stampede.

JEMIMA. And?

LILIA. And your firstborn son. He's . . . dead.

Music: organ bridge.

NARRATOR. *(Voice-over, from the Sony)* Will life get even more trying for Job and his family? Will Kezia emerge from her coma? Will the village surgeons give Keren-happuch the lower jaw she so fervently desires? Will our hero continue to trust God? Tune in tomorrow for the next inspiring episode of *One Man's Misery.*

Job flicks off the Zenith. Franny flicks off the Sony.

FRANNY. Damn. Slept through most of it. I'd better get a clock radio.

JOB. Who the hell are you?

FRANNY. I live here. Franny Fenstermacher. *(Assertive)* This dung is all mine.

JOB. Squatter's rights?

FRANNY. Exactly. *(Friendly but cautious)* I'd be happy to help you find your *own* heap, but this one's taken.

JOB. *(Pointing to cables)* Are you responsible for all these wires and things?

FRANNY. *(Proud)* Uh-huh. Ever visit Fenstermacher's House and Garden Supplies on Central Avenue? I own that too. *(Sweeps hand across dung heap)* I expect I'll install some plumbing next. You know—get the toilet working, maybe put in a Jacuzzi. *(Struggles to her feet, coughing)* Assuming I don't go blind first. The diabetes.

JOB. Oh, dear.

FRANNY. Not to mention the emphysema, the osteoporosis, the arthritis . . .

JOB. How horrible.

FRANNY. It's terrible, but it's not horrible. Horrible's what happened to my husband.

JOB. *(Gulps)* Oh?

FRANNY. Lost everything when our local S & L went under. The day Bill got the news, you know what he did? Walked straight into a McCormick reaper.

JOB. Killed?

FRANNY. Shredded.

JOB. I'm sorry.

FRANNY. Like a CIA document. I can talk about it now, but I nearly went mad at the time.

JOB. Indeed.

FRANNY. Then there's my son. You know what a Bradley-Chambers child is?

JOB. *(Aside)* I don't want to hear about this.

FRANNY. A Bradley-Chambers child suffers from Bradley-Chambers syndrome. Cleft palate, too many fingers, kidneys pitted with lesions, defective heart. He lives in constant pain. My Bradley-Chambers child is named Andy.

JOB. Mercy.

FRANNY. *(Points to the Zenith)* One of these days, Job Barnes is going to get it all back—his possessions, family, health.

JOB. *(Retrieving newspaper)* Not as long as the *ratings* hold up.

FRANNY. Are you being cynical? I don't like cynics. *(Lifts eyes to heaven)* Listen, Lord, I want you to know I'm not bitter. You have your reasons. *(Turns to Job, points skyward)* He has his reasons.

JOB. *(Reads)* "School bus plunges off ravine." *(Turns page)* "Bridge of San Luis Rey collapses." *(Stares at Franny)* Wish I had your faith.

FRANNY. *(Pulls Job's book from apron pocket)* This sustains me. *The Job Barnes Story: How I Suffered, Suppurated, and Survived.* It has a happy ending.

JOB. *(Reads)* "Cholera death toll reaches 15,000 in Iraq." *(Turns page)* "Floods destroy Peruvian village."

FRANNY. Sooner or later, God'll fix everything. He'll heal my child, take away my infirmities, find me a new husband . . .

JOB. And by coming here, you thought you could speed up the process?

FRANNY. *(Defensive)* Is that so crazy? Isn't it logical to suppose he's more likely to notice me if I'm camped out on Job's own dung heap? *(Taps on book)* This all really happened, you know. *The Job Barnes Story* is one hundred percent true.

JOB. *(Nodding)* I wrote it.

FRANNY. *(Shocked)* What?

As Franny consults the author photo on the back of the dust jacket, her jaw drops in astonishment.

FRANNY. Good gracious, that's you! You're Job Barnes! *(Coughs)* I feel so ashamed. Here I am, droning on about my problems to the man who practically *invented* suffering. *(Indicating Job's book)* Says here you lost your herdsmen, your camel drivers, sheep—

JOB. My children.

FRANNY. Oxen, donkeys—and then you got all those awful boils.

JOB. *(Reminiscing)* Scraping myself with a potsherd. Scratching myself to the bone.

FRANNY. The pus oozing out of you like sweat.

JOB. "Curse God and die," Ruth said.

FRANNY. But then you learned to accept. *(Pulls ballpoint pen from apron)* You repented in dust and ashes. *(Thrusts book and pen toward Job)* Hey, do me a favor, Mr. Barnes?

Job takes book and pen from Franny, autographs the title page.

JOB. There. *(Returns book)* A collector's item.

FRANNY. I know what *I'm* doing here, but I don't know what *you're* doing here.

JOB. *(Matter-of-factly)* I want a rematch. I want the debate to continue.

FRANNY. Debate?

JOB. "Resolved: Job Barnes should never have withdrawn his case." *(To heaven)* Got that, sir? I'm back on the old dung heap, and I'm pissed as ever. *(Opens vest-*

pocket Bible, reads) "God destroyeth the perfect and the wicked. If the scourge slay suddenly, he will laugh at the trial of the innocent." Now there's a Job I can respect, keeping his Creator on the hook. *(Flips ahead)* "God hath broken me asunder. He hath taken me by my neck, and shaken me to pieces. He poureth out my gall upon the ground." That's the real me, bloodied but unbowed.

FRANNY. *(Unimpressed)* Okay, but in the end he answered your accusations. He dazzled you with the majesty of the universe. *(Coughs)* He awed you, he amazed you . . .

JOB. He pulled rank on me. *(Reads in Godlike tone)* "Where wast thou when I laid the foundations of the earth?" *(Paraphrasing)* "I'm God, and you're not"—is that an argument, Franny? *(Snaps Bible closed)*

FRANNY. What're you so upset about? He rewarded you handsomely. New family, new house, new herds . . .

JOB. Stock options, trust funds, book royalties, TV residuals. Bribery, all of it. Hush money.

FRANNY. *(Struck by the idea)* Hush money . . .

JOB. Hush camels, hush donkeys: anything to keep me from telling the world how I really felt. He *used* me, Franny. He put me through hell on a dare, then passed it off as an inquiry into the problem of evil. He owes me an apology.

FRANNY. Apology? You're gonna ask God for an *apology?*

JOB. Yup.

FRANNY. Tell you one thing—I'm not planning to be around for that.

JOB. *(To heaven)* Look, sir, we needn't begin with the meat of things. A game of chess will do—I'll give you a bishop advantage and the first move. *(To Franny)* He's not talking. *(To heaven)* Monopoly, sir? Start you out with a hotel on Park Place. Dominoes? Backgammon? *(Reads from Bible)* "Who laid the cornerstone thereof?" *(Sarcastic)* Cornerstone. Earth's cornerstone. Okay, fine, but now let's hear from *today's* God. *(Reads)* "Hast thou given the horse strength? Has thou clothed his neck with thunder?" *(To heaven)* These old metaphors won't do, sir. Not in the post-Darwinian era.

FRANNY. Sometimes, standing in the midday sun with the heat leaping up from these ashes and the flies buzzing in my ears, I can feel it, really feel it. This is hallowed ground, Mr. Barnes.

JOB. *(Selecting a dung nugget)* Shall we take off our shoes?

FRANNY. He's near. He's very near.

JOB. Have you ever considered the taxonomy of turds?

FRANNY. What? *(Offended)* Certainly not.

JOB. At the very bottom: dogshit. The lowest of the low—ragpickers, bag ladies, and people who hang out on dung heaps. When you treat somebody like dogshit, your contempt knows no bounds. *(Tosses the nugget, selects another)* Next we have chickenshit. Chickenshit allows for a certain humanity. A chickenshit may be a disgusting coward, but at least he's not dogshit. *(Tosses the nugget, selects another)* Bullshit comes after that—blatant and aggressive untruths. But at a certain level, of course, we admire our liars, don't we? Bullshitters get elected, chickenshits never. *(Tosses the nugget, selects another)* At the top of the hierarchy, at the summit of the heap: horseshit. Horseshit is false too, but it's not *manifestly* false. Horseshit is subtle. It's nuanced. It plays to win. Horseshit fools some of the people some of the time. Divine justice, for example, is horseshit, not bullshit. Indeed, we hold horseshit in such esteem that we decline to bestow the epithet on one another. A person can be a bullshitter, but only a horse can be a horseshitter.

FRANNY. What a thoroughly depressing person you are. I wish I'd never met you.

A wheelchair rolls into the scene, bearing a thin, pale, thirteen-year-old boy named Tucker, a contemporary equivalent of Tiny Tim. Intravenous feeding tubes lead from his arms to bottles of nutrients set on aluminum poles. Wincing and groaning, he moves the wheels with his gloved hands, gradually maneuvering himself to the base of the dung heap.

FRANNY. Greetings, young man.

Tucker grunts, gasps, and eventually catches his breath.

FRANNY. You okay?

TUCKER. *(Brightly)* Hi, I'm Tucker, and I've got AIDS!

JOB. *(Looking around)* Where are we—Lourdes?

FRANNY. *(To Tucker)* Poor child. Poor, poor child. *(Admonishing Job)* Lourdes was once a dung heap too.

TUCKER. A mislabeled batch of blood, and before I knew it—

FRANNY. You mean you're—

TUCKER. A hemophiliac, ma'am. Dad's about ready to kill himself. Mom's been doin' the talk shows. *(Points to the Zenith)* Hey, does that work? I think she's on at five.

FRANNY. We get a picture on the Zenith, sound on the Sony.

TUCKER. Excellent. Ever watch *One Man's Misery?*

FRANNY. Faithfully.

JOB. First hemophilia, then AIDS. *(To heaven)* My hat goes off to you. You've outdone yourself.

TUCKER. Did I come to the right dung heap? This the place where God appears?

JOB. Every twenty-five hundred years or so. Hope you brought your toothbrush.

FRANNY. You came to exactly the right dung heap.

TUCKER. Are *you* sick, ma'am?

FRANNY. Diabetes.

TUCKER. My aunt had that. Are your legs gonna rot off?

FRANNY. I hope not.

JOB. *(Pointing skyward)* Don't give him any ideas.

TUCKER. *(Indicating Job)* Is he sick too?

FRANNY. He's got hubris.

JOB. Tic-tac-toe, God? Croquet? Clue?

FRANNY. Don't listen to anything he says.

TUCKER. Know what I really hate?

FRANNY. What?

TUCKER. Eggplant. Eggplant and being a virgin. I don't even know what it *looks* like.

FRANNY. Eggplant?

TUCKER. Screwing.

FRANNY. *(Bewildered)* Oh, dear. *(Ponders)* It looks like dancing.

TUCKER. Bullshit.

JOB. Exactly.

TUCKER. Hey, d'ya suppose there're any trading cards around here?

FRANNY. *(Amiably)* I wouldn't be surprised. *(Picks through trash)* Let's go hunting.

Tucker slips a stack of trading cards from his shirt pocket, fanning them out like a bridge hand.

TUCKER. I'm collectin' the series called *Operation Desert Storm.* *(Consults checklist card)* I need "Number Forty-two: Patriot Missile Control Center" and "Number Seventeen: General Colin Powell."

Franny retrieves a cardboard rectangle from the heap.

FRANNY. *(Reads)* "What Pierre Saw Through the Keyhole: Number Thirty-four in a Series of Authentic French Postcards."

TUCKER. Oooo—gimme.

Franny hands Tucker the postcard, then resumes her search.

TUCKER. Golly.

FRANNY. *(Finding Desert Storm card)* Hey, here's one. *(Brings card to Tucker)* Have you got "Number Four: General Norman Schwarzkopf"?

TUCKER. *(Disappointed)* Two of 'em.

FRANNY. My own little boy collects baseball cards. *(Coughs)* That is, he *will* collect baseball cards, after he gets well.

TUCKER. What's his name?

FRANNY. Bradley-Chambers. *(Shudders)* Andy.

JOB. Ping-Pong, God? Tiddlywinks? *(To Franny and Tucker)* Looks like he's closed up shop. Off visiting the fifth planet of Alpha Centauri, dropping brimstone on the natives.

Suddenly the door of the Whirlpool clothes dryer flies open and the barrel begins to turn furiously, spewing socks and underwear across the stage. A calm, soothing, resonant male voice booms out of the chamber.

VOICE FROM THE WHIRLPOOL. *(Slow, measured pace)* Don't be so sure about that . . .

Job and Franny jump three feet into the air and hug each other.

JOB. Jeez!

FRANNY. Gracious!

TUCKER. Wow!

FRANNY. And the Whirlpool isn't even plugged in.

The barrel keeps spinning, generating a strong wind that blows pieces of refuse off the heap and into the audience.

VOICE FROM THE WHIRLPOOL. "Who is this that darkeneth counsel by words without knowledge?"

JOB. *(Fearful)* Er, you d-don't remember me? Your s-servant Job?

As the Voice continues to speak, we feel as if we're in the presence of a bombastic Santa Claus or a lame-duck Southern senator. The Voice certainly doesn't seem malign.

VOICE. "Gird up now thy loins like a man." *(Beat)* Of course I remember you. What's on your mind, son?

TUCKER. *(Points to Job)* He called himself Job. *(Turns to Franny)* Is he really Job?

Nodding, Franny guides Tucker away from the hero. Tucker repockets his trading cards.

FRANNY. Stand over here. I'll explain later.

JOB. Are you the right God? The modern God?

VOICE. I am that I am.

TUCKER. *(To Franny)* He's Popeye the Sailor?

FRANNY. Sshhh.

VOICE. *(Mildly chiding)* Come, come, servant, I haven't got all day.

JOB. I don't intend any disrespect, sir, but . . . may I speak freely?

VOICE. Of course.

JOB. You owe me an apology.

VOICE. A *what?*

JOB. *(Wincing, closing his eyes)* Apology.

Job and Franny brace themselves.

VOICE. I don't do apologies.

JOB. It's like this, sir. The way I see it, you tortured me to win a bet, then proceeded to buy my silence. I guess I'm feeling a bit . . .

VOICE. Exploited?

JOB. Exactly.

VOICE. Used?

JOB. Right.

VOICE. Duped?

JOB. My wife calls me history's patsy.

VOICE. Phooey.

JOB. How's that?

VOICE. I said phooey. *History's* patsy? *(Stifles a chuckle)* You really think the wager ended with you? Let's not be vain, son. The rivalry between God and Satan goes on forever—rather like that crummy soap opera you all watch. Remember the bubonic plague?

JOB. Who could forget?

VOICE. My way of testing Samuel Schechner, a singularly pious rug merchant living in fourteenth-century London.

FRANNY. *(Confused)* Huh? The whole plague? For one Jew?

VOICE. The whole plague. For one Jew.

TUCKER. Gosh.

VOICE. Then there was polio. Satan and I wanted to see if Franklin Delano Roosevelt would curse me to my face.

FRANNY. *(Perturbed)* You created polio just for *that?*

VOICE. Uh-huh.

FRANNY. Goodness.

VOICE. The 1982 Colombian earthquake? I was challenging the faith of Juan Delgado, a prosperous coffee merchant living in Bogata. As for diabetes and emphysema—yes, Franny, they exist for the sole and holy purpose of permitting you to demonstrate your devotion to me.

FRANNY. I'm trying my best.

VOICE. Finally, of course, there's AIDS. A major pestilence, sure, but no match for the grit and gumption of young Tucker here.

TUCKER. *(Unconvinced)* Er, you bet . . .

FRANNY. *(Coughs)* He's only thirteen.

TUCKER. Thirteen and a half.

JOB. How many of these showdowns have there been?

VOICE. Enough to keep my job interesting.

FRANNY. *(Insistent)* How many?

VOICE. Four thousand, seven hundred and fifty-eight.

FRANNY. And the score?

VOICE. Behold!

The number 4,758 materializes on the Zenith TV, the numeral 0 on the Sony.

VOICE. God: four thousand, seven hundred and fifty-eight. Satan: zero.

TUCKER. That old Devil's a glutton for punishment.

VOICE. *(Agreeing)* He never learns.

FRANNY. *(Apprehensive)* And in every case, you restored the victim to health, wealth, and happiness?

VOICE. Maybe not in *every* case.

FRANNY. *(Indignant, to Tucker)* I think he owes all those people an apology.

VOICE. What was that, Franny?

FRANNY. *(To clothes dryer)* I said . . . you owe all those people an apology. *(Steels herself, closes eyes)* Has he incinerated us yet?

JOB. Not yet.

VOICE. I'll make you a deal, Franny. I won't tell you how to run your hardware store, and you won't tell me how to run the universe. "Where wast thou when I laid the foundations of the earth? Who laid the cornerstone thereof?"

JOB. *(Contemptuous)* Don't give us your flat-earth theory. *(Brandishing a turd)* Don't give us your geocentric solar system, your pre-Darwinian biology, or any of that crap.

FRANNY. That horseshit.

JOB. Right.

VOICE. *(Condescending but not vicious)* Hey, you made some progress recently. Great. I'm happy for you. But maybe *I've* been busy too. Maybe, a couple thousand years ago, maybe I added an afterlife. Follow what I'm saying? In one corner we have *you* people, klutzing around with your science, and meanwhile here's the Creator, solving death itself. Don't come whining to me about diabetes and AIDS when I'm doling out immortality, okay?

JOB. We don't want justice in *heaven*.

FRANNY. We want it on the dung heap.

TUCKER. He's not a very *nice* clothes dryer.

FRANNY. He's putting us through the ringer.

JOB. *(Fully the accuser now)* Does the name Naomi Barnes mean anything to you?

VOICE. Who?

JOB. Naomi Barnes.

VOICE. *(Slightly chagrined)* I've created so many people . . .

JOB. She was one of those seven sons and three daughters I had in the beginning. Chapter One, Verse Nineteen. *(Quavering)* She had a name. A face.

FRANNY. Freckles?

JOB. No freckles.

FRANNY. Andy has freckles.

VOICE. Ah, so you want to quote scripture, eh, bigshot? Let's move on up to Chapter Forty-two. Suddenly you've got seven brand-new sons and three brand-new daughters, just as good as the old ones. Better in fact. "And in all the land were no women found so fair as the daughters of Job."

FRANNY. He's never going to apologize, is he?

JOB. It's not in his nature.

Franny sits down on the dung heap, thoroughly discouraged.

VOICE. You know what I like about you folks? You're so *innocent*. And around here innocence gets rewarded. Go ahead, name your price. You want a house in the country?

JOB. My herdsmen were innocent too.

VOICE. A Lear jet? Superbowl tickets?

FRANNY. *(Rising as she coughs and shakes fist)* His shepherds were innocent.

VOICE. A table at Sardi's? A castle in Spain?

FRANNY. *(Coughing)* Give this man his self-respect back! Give this boy his future back!

VOICE. *(Slightly paranoid)* "Where wast thou when I laid the foundations of the earth?"

JOB. *(Rolling his eyes)* Here we go again.

FRANNY. One-track mind.

Franny hobbles over to the Zenith TV. Rooting around in the junk, she draws out a can of red paint and an artist's brush.

JOB. That's the idea!

TUCKER. Go for it!

VOICE. "Who shut up the sea with doors, when it brake forth, as if it had issued out of the womb? Hast thou commanded the morning since thy days?"

Slowly, methodically, Franny crosses out the 4,758 on the Zenith screen and replaces it with 4,755, then changes the 0 on the Sony to a 3. Job and Tucker applaud.

VOICE. *(Furious)* "Hast thou entered into the springs of the sea? Hast thou seen the doors of the shadow of death? And the hoary frost of heaven: who hath engendered it?"

The clothes dryer barrel spins madly, generating a fearsome tornado that begins tearing the dung heap apart.

VOICE. *(Raging)* "Canst thou bind the sweet influences of Pleiades, or loose the bands of Orion? Knowest thou the ordinances of heaven? Canst thou send lightnings, that they may go, and say unto thee, 'Here we are'?"

JOB. And now it's time . . .

FRANNY. To curse God . . .

JOB. And live.

The lights go out. The stage is dark but for the glowing scoreboards. God: 4,755. Satan: 3.

JOB. Go to hell, clothes dryer!

FRANNY. Eat worms, clothes dryer!

TUCKER. Your sister's ugly, clothes dryer!

The three mortals continue hurling out curses, voices blending in a cacophony of rage.

JOB. Go to hell!

FRANNY. Eat worms!

TUCKER. Your sister's ugly!

JOB. Hell!

FRANNY. Worms!

TUCKER. Ugly!

The storm grows quiet. The lights come up. Job and Franny are nearly nude now, their garments torn off by the wind. Wads of trash cling to their flesh. The clothes dryer is still and empty.

TUCKER. Hey, you guys are *naked!*

JOB. "Naked came I out of my mother's womb . . ."

FRANNY. "And naked shall I return thither . . ."

TUCKER. Will you show me what screwing looks like?

FRANNY. Right now we just want to get out of here.

TUCKER. Where're we goin'?

JOB. I don't know. East. We're looking for something.

TUCKER. What?

JOB. Better major appliances.

TUCKER. Anything else?

FRANNY. "Number Forty-two: Patriot Missile Control Center."

JOB. "Number Seventeen: General Colin Powell."

FRANNY. I hear Frigidaire has a good product line.

JOB. I'm told you can't go wrong with a Maytag.

Tucker pulls his trading cards from his shirt. Job and Franny join hands and together they start to wheel Tucker away.

TUCKER. *(Studying checklist card)* How about "Number Fifty-one: Ready for Takeoff"?

JOB. We'll find one.

TUCKER. And "Number Six: Secretary of Defense Dick Cheney"?

JOB. Sure, Tucker.

TUCKER. It's pretty rare.

FRANNY. So are you, kid.

Job, Franny, and Tucker disappear offstage. Their voices drift across the ruins of the dung heap.

TUCKER. "Number Twenty-three: Midair Refueling"?

JOB. Of course.

TUCKER. "Number Thirty-five: Bombs Over Baghdad"?

FRANNY. Naturally.

TUCKER. "Number Fifty-eight: Burning Oil Wells"?

JOB. Right.

TUCKER. "Number Sixty-five: Mission Accomplished"?

FRANNY. Yeah . . .

Lights fade out.

Curtain.

Diary of a Mad Deity

❖

OCTOBER 17, 1999

I AWOKE in a strange place. A dark window, speckled with rain, loomed over me like a diseased mirror. The bed was a kind of minimalist arena, large and sunken; I found myself imagining an audience around the perimeter, awaiting the start of some pornographic sports event. I pushed back the silk sheets—what was all this costing me?—and stumbled to the window, staring down at the galaxy of lights. Manhattan? Yes, there stood the World Trade Center, there the Empire State Building. I could even see my old stomping ground, Queens. At least I hadn't left town. Dawn washed across the city like slow surf.

"Hello, Jack."

A soft, purring voice, as if from a larynx soaked in

honey. I turned. On the bed lay a svelte, large-lipped brunette dressed in nothing but a sheet.

"Ready for another hayride?" the woman asked, patting the mattress. "Now I know why they call you Jack, darling. You could lift a Winnebago with that lever of yours."

It is all preposterous, of course. I am no Don Juan, and my name, as you well know, dearest diary, is Gunther Black. In the last year, people have tried to pin "Jeremy Green," "Thomas Brown," and most improbably, "Ernest Red" on me. Jack? That was a new one.

"Where are we?" I asked.

"Park Avenue. The Mayfair Regent. Your treat, remember?" Alarmed, the woman tore the sheet away. "*I'm* certainly not paying for it." Her nipples stared at me accusingly.

"Park Avenue?" I didn't remember leaving SoHo. "Really?" I blinked the murk from my eyes. Oriental rug, crystal chandelier, large-screen TV, a champagne bottle buried to the neck in cracked ice: Jack had taste, I'd give him that. My pants were draped across a velour sofa. A few seconds of fumbling produced my wallet. I pulled out two twenties and let them flutter to the mattress like origami birds. "Send out for some breakfast," I said, dressing. "Don't worry, I'll pay for the room."

"I should hope so, Jack."

I never even learned her name.

OCTOBER 18, 1999

Another nightmare about my sister. Brittany and I are in a besieged snow fort. Bloody corpses brush our knees. Snowballs fly toward us like grapeshot canisters. "I hope summer comes soon," Brittany says.

"Tomorrow," I tell her.

A fearsome ice ball sails over the rampart and strikes her neck. The impact is incredible, cutting through flesh, vertebrae, spinal cord. Her severed head hits a snowdrift, staining the whiteness.

"Tomorrow will be too late," her head explains.

OCTOBER 20, 1999

After three cups of coffee and an hour watching the Comedy Channel, I finally got a good start on the new novel, tentatively titled *Antichrist*. Jesus returns, only it's really Satan in disguise. He gets elected president of the United States by a landslide and turns the White House into a den of perversion, torture, murder, and sadism.

My editor wants to cash in on the millennium.

I compose my rough drafts on legal pads. My desk is an upended closet door supported by cinder blocks. Why? What is wrong with me? For years now I've been making enough to buy a computer and move uptown, but the maddening leaks in my bank account keep me stuck in this cockroach preserve on Third Street, writing on a door. The building styles itself an artists' community, so I should feel at home. I don't. Around here an artist is someone who fashions ten-foot-high phalli from poured concrete, performs in scorched-earth experimental theater, or creates "nonfigurative television" out of synthesized feedback and multilated videotape. An author of paperback novels for Dungeon Press is automatically consigned to the *arrière garde*.

Even after my recent successes—three best-sellers in as many years—I would still rather edit horror novels than write them, but so far no house has kept me for more than a month. I am told that I abuse the authors, writing cruel remarks on their manuscripts. I don't.

Except I do, apparently—during my "fugue states," as Dr. Izzard terms my bouts of amnesia. Tuneless fugues, these. Helplessly I carom between the Scylla of remembered nightmare and the Charybdis of forgotten action. My loft overflows with clothes I did not buy, parking tickets I did not earn, and yogurt of unknown origin. A strange calico cat paces around on my makeshift desk, wearing our mutual address on her collar. Magazines to which I did not subscribe arrive regularly, bearing the names of Jeremy Green, Thomas Brown, and Ernest Red. Evidently these men have nothing in common: Jeremy takes *Mother Jones*, Thomas gets *Forbes*, and Mr. Red—wouldn't you know?—is a *Guns and Ammo* reader. How long before "Jack" gets hold of my address? How long before *Crotch Shots* appears in my mailbox?

For six months I've been bringing Dr. Izzard my complaints: blackouts, nightmares, headaches, insomnia, appetite loss. On Friday, finally, he'll give me his "pre-liminary diagnosis." My own preliminary diagnosis is that I am out of my skull and getting farther from its vicinity every day.

OCTOBER 21, 1999

We are in a pumpkin patch, selecting a future jack-o'-lantern. Brittany alights on a gigantic specimen, a kind of organic boulder, and stabs it with her penknife. No subconscious invention here—Brittany was a girl who knew about knives.

The pumpkin is Pandora's box. Hideous creatures rush out—hornets, dragonflies, bats, ropes of fibrous black smoke—falling on Brittany with carnivorous zeal, shucking the flesh from her bones.

Last time it was a snowball, before that a sea urchin, before that the globular head of a medieval mace. Why is my sister always killed by a sphere?

OCTOBER 22, 1999

This has been the strangest day of my life. My lives, I should say, if I interpret my illness correctly.

A headache hit me like a jackhammer breaking into my cranium. I collapsed on Izzard's plush velvet couch. Then: nothingness. Then: "Gunther, is that you?"

"Who else?"

"I'm with Gunther now, correct?" Izzard took a long puff. I had spent the morning trying to cleanse *Antichrist* of clichés only to find myself talking to a psychiatrist with a pipe. "Listen, Gunther, what I'm about to tell you will sound bizarre and perhaps frightening."

"It's hopeless," I said. "I'm insane."

"Hopeless? No. *Rare,* certainly. No more than two hundred cases ever reported." Izzard puffed. I don't believe he enjoys tobacco, but he loves collecting pipes whose bowls are sculpted to resemble movie stars. Today he is smoking Peter Lorre, an actor whose roundish features and poached-egg eyes might have informed the prototype of Izzard himself. "You are certainly not insane. I believe you suffer from dissociation—a severe but treatable psychoneurosis. You've heard of Dr. Jekyll and Mr. Hyde?"

Had the Pope heard of the Virgin Mary? "I'm a horror writer, remember?" An odd thrill wove through me. I was deranged, but romantically deranged: a good, old-fashioned Gothic monster, hobbling along London's cobblestone streets, serpents of fog entwining my bent frame and fractured psyche. "One of my favorites."

"Stevenson did a remarkable job of anticipating the syndrome, but he got one thing wrong." Izzard's accent also owes something to Peter Lorre, a mildly depraved European wheeze. "Jekyll knew about Hyde's comings and goings, whereas in actual split-personality cases the parasites so resent the body's true owner that they refuse to enter his consciousness. Do I make sense?" A Möbius strip of smoke rose from my therapist's pipe. "In the last few weeks I've met Jeremy Green, Thomas Brown, Ernest

Red, and Jack Silver—introduced them to each other, discussed your case with them. They will always remain strangers to you. You will know them only through inference."

"Through their magazine subscriptions, you mean? The food they leave in the refrigerator?"

"Exactly."

I was on the upswing of a roller-coaster plunge, at the point where one's stomach is riding several feet above one's heart: dizzy, yet glad to be beyond the worst. "This is hard to absorb."

"Naturally."

"Split, you said. I sound shattered."

"Multiple, we call it. You're a multiple."

A multiple. The beast had a name. I had met the enemy and he was I. No, *they*—Jeremy and Thomas and the others to whom I was host. "I'd rather be insane."

Izzard switched the burning Peter Lorre for a cold Spencer Tracy. "I'll give you some articles to read, the famous cases—Ansel Bourne, Sally Beauchamp, Billy Milligan. A few became popular books, but most are only in the professional literature." He slid back a file drawer and, after rummaging around, drew out an issue of the *Journal of Abnormal Psychology*. "As I recall, Sybil Dorsett's life was done on flat-screen television in the seventies, and Joanne Woodward got an Academy Award for *The Three Faces of Eve*. Both stories had happy endings, Gunther. The patients were cured."

I took the magazine, dated winter of 1993. A multiple personality named Felix Bass had made the cover. "My others—what are they like?"

"From what he's told me, I would describe Jeremy Green as a left-wing intellectual. Thomas Brown is a Christian fundamentalist with generally conservative leanings. Ernest Red is a ruffian who fancies himself a big-game hunter and soldier of fortune. Jack Silver—ever wake up with an inexplicable hangover?"

"Often."

"Jack gave them to you. A hedonist." Izzard filled Spencer Tracy with tobacco, tamped it down. Am I wise to entrust my remaining shreds of sanity to this odd little gnome? "Our goal will be to integrate your separate selves into a single consciousness, someone who has command of his predecessors' memories." He lit his pipe. "To do that we must first locate the root of your dissociation."

"You'll hypnotize me?"

"Hypnosis is a blunt, inelegant tool—I can see why Freud abandoned it. Dream analysis will get us much further. Mere talking will get us furthest of all."

"You know about my nightmares."

"They always end with your sister's death, correct?"

"Always."

"In truth she was murdered."

I had told him the story twice already. "Stabbed by some punks in Kissena Park," I said, clipping each syllable, hoping he sensed my impatience.

"The multiple personality typically suffers from unconscious hatred against a family member. Usually a parent, sometimes a sibling."

"I loved my sister."

"I don't doubt it." Izzard gave Spencer Tracy an emphatic puff. "But only after draining the swamp of your inner life will we have enough solid ground on which to construct the new you—the healed, controlling, omniscient ego."

"The new me. And what about the *old* me?"

"It will disappear."

"Sounds like murder."

"No, Gunther. Birth."

OCTOBER 26, 1999

This afternoon I fell asleep trying to provide *Antichrist* with a Chapter Three. A Brittany dream came—the first I've ever had during the daytime.

We are in a private swimming pool, romping in the turquoise water. A beach ball glides into my hands. "Throw it here," Brittany calls. I comply. As her arms cradle the ball, it explodes like a grenade, leaving an archipelago of blood on the water.

I awoke. Chapter Three hovered before me, scrawled in ballpoint on my legal pad. ". . . as Lucifer's talons, slashing across her bodice, revealed the lush, forbidden fruits he had craved so long."

Which is where I had stopped. The text, however, continued:

YOU WILL NEVER GET RID OF US, GUNTHER BLACK.
YOU ARE OUTNUMBERED BEYOND HOPE.
GIVE UP.

OCTOBER 29, 1999

Today Izzard decided to administer Rorschach tests to my other selves. "Let me talk to Thomas, please," he said, opening a spiral-bound notebook on his knees.

Was that all it took to evoke one of these characters? Unlikely, I thought.

A migraine sawed through my skull.

Fugue state . . .

Coming out of it, I immediately sensed Izzard's distress. His hands lay folded on his lap in a tight, lumpy bundle. Grotesque cartoon faces were doodled across two adjacent pages in his notebook.

"What's the problem?" I asked.

"Am I talking to Gunther now?" Izzard demanded. Even from the couch, I could see that each cartoon face bore a name. "Gunther?"

"Of course."

"Good."

"Don't tell me—they all flunked the Rorschach."

"I never administered it," Izzard confessed. The cartoon faces wore varied expressions. A few smiled. Many frowned. One shed tears. Another had an elaborate grid of teeth, his lips pulled into a grimace. "I couldn't. Others kept emerging, personalities I hadn't met before."

"Others." The word stuck in my throat like a burr.

Izzard scanned his notes. "Amos Indigo. A real bohemian, I'd say. Currently writing a short story about a talking calico cat. Leon Mauve, a homosexual with a passion for midnight screenings of cult films."

"That explains the ticket stubs."

"Alexander Yellow. A blatant racist, I'm sorry to report. Bernie Gold, however, plans to write an exposé of antisemitism in America."

I attempted to smile, lost heart at midpoint. "So, including me, we've got nine, right? I have nine heads, like the Hydra."

Izzard gulped. Repression is not a soothing sign in a psychiatrist.

"You're not finished, are you?" I said.

He flipped a notebook page: dozens of faces, each with a name and a characteristic countenance. "It's surely the most baroque case ever reported. Sybil Dorsett had seventeen personalities altogether. You've got . . ." He fixed on his notes. "William Orange, Roger Vermilion, Jason Gray, Peter Pink, Ilene Amber, Judith Fuchsia . . . I'll be candid, Gunther. A total of fifty-nine separate selves appeared today. And there may be more."

"Fifty-nine?"

"Fifty-nine."

"Jesus. Ilene, you said? And Judith? I have *women* inside me?"

"If you believe Carl Jung," said Izzard, "we all have women inside us."

NOVEMBER 23, 1999

This morning I read the first five chapters of *Antichrist,* a hundred pages coated with ballpoint scrawl. They are uniformly awful. It is hard to believe that the man who wrote *Sermons by Satan* and *Cacodaemon* perpetrated this tripe.

NOVEMBER 5, 1999

I awoke at three A.M. Brittany and I had been drifting over Queens in a hot-air balloon. A rope had broken, the basket had tilted, and my sister had fallen into the sky . . .

"You're certain it was your sister?" Izzard asked during our session.

"Positive."

"Her death, her real death—let me hear about it once more."

I flattened myself against the couch. "It's a horrible story."

"How old was she?"

"Fourteen."

"And you?"

"Ten. We lived in Queens, a Corona Avenue apartment near 108th Street." So there I was, tricked by Izzard into telling it again. "One of those hot summer nights when the air feels like a snail's skin. Mom sent us to buy milk. A safe neighborhood—streetlamps, lots of cops. It should have been okay, but Brittany insisted we hike home through the park. I really don't like talking about this."

"Kissena Park?"

"Kissena. Right. Suddenly something catches Brittany's eye, and she charges away. A full moon, but I still can't find her, not anywhere. Finally I run home. Dad has to slap me before I stop crying. He calls the police, and then everybody goes to the park, and they spot her about an hour later. It took them a while because the bushes were so dense. Two dozen stab wounds."

"Did you see the corpse?"

"Not that night, only at the funeral. By then they'd covered her with cosmetics."

"And the cops decided it was punks?" Strange to hear *cops* and *punks* from Izzard's Continental tongue.

"They questioned the local gangs. The Rodman Street Goons, the Corona Avenue Nightwings . . . a few others, I don't remember the names."

"The cops came up empty?"

"They never even found the knife. Who would expect it? The punks just threw it in Flushing Bay, right?"

Izzard's whole body became a frown. "Gunther, I have reached a conclusion. The analysis cannot proceed until we know *exactly* how many personalities inhabit you. Dawn-to-dusk sessions are not normally a useful technique, but in your case . . ."

"All day? I could never afford that."

"I have a sliding scale. Like a parking garage."

I pictured Izzard running a parking garage, speeding

away in his customers' catatonic Volvos and manic-depressive Saabs, presenting them with sane cars at day's end. "All right," I told him. "Dawn-to-dusk."

NOVEMBER 9, 1999

Antichrist is hopeless. Satan's White House orgies are derivative and ludicrous. In Chapter Fourteen the real Jesus will appear and team up with Richard Nixon's ghost, the two of them forming a kind of ectoplasmic hit squad out to get Satan. This sounds promising, but I can't seem to write the intervening scenes.

The woman down the hall makes concrete phalli. We do not communicate. The young male misanthrope on the third floor writes poems without words in them. I have nothing to say to him. When a man suffers from dissociation and writer's block, dearest diary, he needs friends.

NOVEMBER 14, 1999

When Izzard said dawn-to-dusk, he wasn't kidding. He insisted that I meet him at six A.M. All this special effort—my case must really fascinate him. Perhaps he's envisioning one of those multiple-personality cover stories for the *Journal of Abnormal Psychology,* or maybe he wants to take me to the upcoming International Psychoanalytic Association congress in Bonn. Look, *sehr geehrten Doktoren,* behold this most curious fish. It didn't get away.

Izzard had brought coffee and donuts. We feasted,

and then he said, "I'd like to speak to William Orange now."

"Is that really all it takes?"

A volcano erupted in my brain, the lava smothering my resented self.

Fugue state . . .

And suddenly I was asking, "What did you discover?" Odd. Izzard had claimed we would go till evening, yet ripe sunlight poured through the window. "It didn't take as long as you thought?"

"Longer," Izzard muttered, loading his Frederic March pipe.

"Longer?" I marveled at how Izzard could stretch out on the floor with so little loss of dignity. Scraps of paper, each decorated with notes and doodled faces, encircled his recumbent form.

"It's Sunday morning," he said.

"Sunday morning? Are you serious?" He was. My vacant stomach tugged at me. Exhaustion hung on my bones. "Let's get it over with. How many?"

Izzard lit Frederic March. "In your case, the sheer quantity of selves may be less relevant than—"

"How *many?*" I insisted.

"It's difficult to say," snapped Izzard, his tone clarifying who the therapist was in this case, who the patient. "Some of your selves reported the existence of personalities whom I failed to draw out. In other instances, I was told of personalities who sounded so innocuous that I decided against soliciting them."

"Just give me an estimate, Dr. Izzard. I'm going to burst."

"If I absolutely had to put a number on it, I would say about . . . well, three thousand."

"Three *thousand?*"

"Give or take a dozen."

"That's preposterous."

"They kept flipping past, one damn persona after the other. It was like scanning the Manhattan phone book." Izzard began sketching Frankenstein stitches on his doodles. "The really interesting feature is the organizational scheme that's emerging. As you may know, Gunther, the human family is truly a family. Everyone on earth is everyone else's fiftieth cousin—if not closer. So it's not surprising that certain personalities are claiming blood kinship to each other and grouping themselves into surname categories."

"Surname categories? I have families inside of me?"

"The Greens, the Silvers, the Siennas, the Pinks . . ."

"Be honest. This is bad news, isn't it?"

"Not necessarily. Remember, our goal is to fuse your various selves into a ruling ego. Within a given family, the challenge of assimilation should prove no harder than in a conventional multiple-personality case. Between families, however, we must contend with feuding, religious intolerance, ethnic pride, and similar schisms."

"I'm crazy as a bedbug, aren't I?"

"Complex, Gunther. You are very, very complex."

NOVEMBER 19, 1999

Voices chatter within me, a cacophony of failed communication and successful disgust. My liberals scream at my conservatives. My racists spew epithets at my minorities. My fundamentalist Protestants condemn my Catholics to hell.

"Voices, Dr. Izzard. I'm hearing voices. Schizophrenics hear voices."

"How do you feel about these voices?"

"They scare the crap out of me."

"Good." Izzard opened my file and removed a sheaf of doodled faces. "A true psychotic does not fear his voices. He takes them for granted. It never even occurs to him that they might indicate madness. You, on the other hand, have the reaction of a sane person. I'm most encouraged."

"The reaction of a sane person suffering from history's worst case of dissociation."

"Perhaps."

"Can you make them stop?"

"I don't know." Izzard drew halos above several faces. "I think we should go back to your sister's death."

"We did that last week."

"Tell me again."

I spoke at twice normal speed. Walking with Brittany through Kissena Park. Her disappearance. The screams. My flight. The terrible funeral . . .

"You heard screams?" Izzard interrupted.

"Yes."

"You never mentioned screams before."

NOVEMBER 22, 1999

Screams. I would settle for mere screams now, wouldn't I? Mere screams would be soothing compared with recent developments.

When my inquisitors burn my heretics, I feel the flames in my heart. When my bigots lynch my blacks, my windpipe constricts and I fall gasping to the floor.

Call it psychosomatic, but it hurts.

NOVEMBER 24, 1999

I have become a sleepwriter. I doze off upon the couch and awaken in the dinette, a ballpoint pen in my hand, a legal pad pressed against my chest like a poultice. I cannot identify the various flags, national seals, military insignia, and infantry uniforms littering the pad, but the renderings have indisputable flair. Even the income tax forms boast a certain elegance.

My favorite flag depicts a rainbow arcing like a flying buttress between two mountain peaks. Most inspiring.

Clearly I have hidden talent.

NOVEMBER 25, 1999

Insomnia.

A walk through Washington Square.

Lighting flared everywhere, revealing a circle of Caucasian males in eighteenth-century greatcoats whipping a naked, dark-skinned, aboriginal woman.

When I got home, I found welts on my back.

NOVEMBER 27, 1999

Saturday. Another dawn-to-dusk session. This one, at least, truly ended at dusk.

"You've gone political," Izzard announced when I had regained myself. "The families have started forming . . . well, as you might imagine . . ."

"I know all about it. Countries, right?"

"You've got countries," Izzard corroborated in the tone of a blunt but compassionate internist offering a diagnosis of AIDS. "And, naturally, alliances of countries. There's a communist pact, a free enterprise treaty, and a collection of poor, developing nations that view both blocs with grave suspicion."

What can a man do under such circumstances but laugh? "I don't need a psychiatrist, Dr. Izzard, I need a diplomatic corps."

Instead of echoing my laughter, Izzard offered a smile of corroboration, as if I had taken the words from his mouth. "I spent most of this afternoon talking with the secretary of state from Sovereigntia and the foreign minister from Proletaria." His earnestness left me impossibly depressed. "Gunther, it is my sad duty to inform you that, come midnight, a state of war will exist between your two superpowers."

NOVEMBER 28, 1999

Izzard called to ask how I'm doing—and to cancel next Friday's session. A therapists' convention in Philadelphia.

"The war has begun," I told him.

DECEMBER 9, 1999

War. I look in the mirror and behold an amalgam of cancer patient and auto-accident victim. The main theater is above my shoulders. Bombs detonate, and my vision blurs. Shells explode, and my teeth rattle, sometimes working free of my skull. A patrol is ambushed, and the blood rolls from my ears and nose. Both sides are using mustard gas. My cough has become one continuous convulsion. I am as bald as Izzard.

In my torso, a second front has opened. My nipples drip pus. I quiver with third-degree burns, raw and weeping, black craters on the landscape of my chest.

The emergency staffs at Beth Israel Hospital and NYU Medical Center know me on sight. I am running out of lies.

DECEMBER 10, 1999

"My God," said Izzard, beholding my torn and leaking self. Normally unflappable, he could not watch me without flinching.

"Help me," I bleated.

"I'll try. Believe me, I'll try." He guided me toward the couch, eased me onto its understanding plush. "I assume you're getting medical attention?"

"The best an emergency room can offer."

"We'll cancel today's session if—"

"No!" How pathetic I must have sounded. Yes, Doc, I know I'm doomed, but give me some of your prettiest pills anyway. "Please!"

"I think we should talk about those nightmares again. Your sister is always killed by a sphere, correct?"

"Always." With my tongue I probed a gap between two of my extant teeth.

Izzard procured a fat manila envelope from his top desk drawer, resting it on my chest. I opened it, and a dozen photographs tumbled out.

"Study them," Izzard urged.

A snowball, a pumpkin, a hot-air balloon, a melon, the moon, a large female breast, a buttock of indeterminate gender, a globe, the Perisphere from the 1940 New York World's Fair, the Unisphere from the 1965 New York World's Fair, a soccer ball, an apple.

I reversed the exhibit. Apple, soccer ball, Unisphere. My intestines became a *Laocoön,* a mass of murdering serpents. "This one," I groaned, shoving the Unisphere toward Izzard.

"It distresses you?" he asked.

"Yes."

"Why?"

"I don't know. Because it's a sphere?" A cough ripped through the delicate netting of my lungs.

"Every picture I showed you is a sphere." Izzard stuck the Unisphere in my file. "I would like to speak with Donald Puce," he said abruptly.

"Who the hell is that?"

"Director of international security policy for Sovereigntia's Department of Defense. Just give him to me, Gunther. The situation is deteriorating rapidly."

Headache . . .

Fugue state . . .

"Exactly as I feared," said Izzard after I was restored to myself.

"What is?"

"You're not going to like it."

"I don't like anything you tell me these days."

"It would appear that . . ."

"Yes?"

"It would appear that Sovereigntia and Proletaria have both started crash programs to develop a thermonuclear bomb."

DECEMBER 13, 1999

I black out constantly. *Antichrist* is a lost cause. I awaken to find my diary defaced.

CAPITALIST PIG!

COLLECTIVIST BASTARD!

WE SHALL DANCE ON YOUR GRAVE!

WE SHALL EXHUME YOUR CORPSE AND SPIT ON IT!

DECEMBER 17, 1999

The rumors are true. Izzard has checked and rechecked, talking with dozens of high-level officials in my Politburo.

Proletaria has the bomb. Bombs, actually. Dozens of them, plus delivery systems. If Sovereigntia does not surrender unconditionally within the next seventy-two hours, an all-out attack will ensue.

"An all-out attack?" I said, shivering with the pain of my newest burns. "What the hell does that mean?"

"I'm not sure," Izzard replied. "But when I look at what *conventional* war has done to you, Gunther, I incline toward a grave prognosis. I pray that Sovereigntia sues for peace."

"This is crazy." A dribble of blood exited my right nostril. "It's like I'm committing suicide."

"True, true."

"What can we do?"

Izzard offered his handkerchief. "I want to delve into your Unisphere phobia."

"I'm about to blow myself up, and you want to talk about the 1965 New York World's Fair?"

"Normally I would have you free-associate over the course of several sessions until the truth popped up. But time is—"

"I'm dying." I pressed the handkerchief against my nose.

Ever so slightly, Izzard nodded. "We must act quickly. For all its crudity, hypnosis is our best card now. So with your permission . . ."

"Do it."

No hypnotic crystals, no gold watch swaying before my eyes. Izzard merely told me to relax. Fat chance, I thought, but the gnome persisted, and finally the world dropped away. . . .

And I slept. . . .

And slept. . . .

And the world came back. . . .

Izzard's eyes, those popping gelatinous transplants from Peter Lorre, told all.

"You've learned something," I said accusingly.

"You will too, shortly. During your trance, I instructed you to recall the whole scene, every detail of your sister's murder, the moment I tap on the desk."

Izzard pulled Spencer Tracy from his mouth.

Every detail? Did I want that?

Izzard inverted the pipe, using it as a mallet. *Tap, tap, tap*.

Floodgates opened, releasing not water but my mind's foulest effluvium. . . .

Brittany and I hurry through the nocturnal park.

Moonlight.

Thick summer air.

"What park?" Izzard demanded.

"Kissena Park in Queens. You know all about it."

"Might it have been Flushing Meadow Park?"

"Kissena, Flushing Meadow—they're contiguous. What's the difference?"

Something catches Brittany's eye. She runs. I begin my fruitless search. Her screams come. They are wild and oddly metallic. They crack the moon. I turn and run. . . .

"Home?" Izzard asked.

"Yes," I said.

"No," Izzard insisted.

"No?" I winced. Izzard was right. "Deeper into Flushing Meadow Park," I said.

Flushing Meadow Park. Site of the 1965 New York World's Fair.

"I see the Unisphere," I told Izzard. "But it is 1970."

"They kept the Unisphere after the fair closed," Izzard explained.

So I truly see it. A huge hollow globe flashing blue-white in the full moon, seven continental slabs affixed to its weblike shell.

The screams have stopped.

Four boys, youthful monsters in thrall to God-knows-what narcotic, stand inside the Unisphere, balancing on the network of steel girders. They have hauled Brittany up with them. Her clothes are gone. I have never seen all her skin before. She is supine and spread-eagled, tied to the back of Argentina, a bandanna on each wrist and ankle, another in her mouth.

I am ten. I do not understand. One gang member seems to be getting dressed. Another is lowering his trousers. From the posture he assumes, I believe he intends to urinate on her. Then he presses forward, kneading her breasts. I avert my eyes. I seem to hear my sister's bones grinding against Argentina. At last I look up. Another boy is doing the same terrible thing. He finishes. A third boy works himself into her, laughing as she rolls and twists on the torture rack that is the world.

And now, suddenly, I do understand, because knives have appeared, flashing in the moonlight.

"I've seen enough," I told Izzard.

"Not quite," he replied.

The knives enter her quivering flesh from everywhere, and blood spills out, quarts of it, staining the continent's underside, blood on Argentina, blood on Chile, now raining through the vast interstice called the South Atlantic . . .

And I am off, running, tearing out of Flushing Meadow Park, careening wildly down Roosevelt Avenue, my psyche a breeding ground for dissociation.

"Shattered," I said.

"Shattered," Izzard agreed.

So now you know why I ripped Izzard's couch apart this morning, dearest diary. He was polite about it. He simply carried his wastebasket over and filled it with the scattered gobs of stuffing and upholstery. "The question, of course, is where this gets us," he said.

I made no reply.

"Knowing the source of a multiple's dissociation is only the beginning," said Izzard.

I pulled more stuffing from the couch, wadding it as if molding a snowball.

"I'll tell you where I think this gets us, though I don't like it," Izzard confessed.

I remained silent.

"Weeks ago, Gunther, I informed you that a multiple typically suffers from repressed hatred. Normally the object of that hatred is a family member. In your case, however, the nemesis lies elsewhere. I believe your psychoneurosis is focused on . . . do you want to know the object?"

I said nothing.

"Gunther, your psychoneurosis is focused on the Unisphere in Flushing Meadow Park . . . and everything it stands for."

DECEMBER 19, 1999

So I hate the world. There is no hope. Proletaria has the bomb, and I hate myself, the world.

The voices know it. Their chatter has decayed into a single wail coursing through my brain. Tomorrow, despite Izzard's noble effort to cure me, I shall hold a nuclear revolver to my temple and pull the trigger.

DECEMBER 20, 1999

YOU WILL NEVER GET RID OF US, GUNTHER BLACK, OUR BOMBS ARE INEVITABLE, BUT YOU ARE NOT.

TEN . . . NINE . . . EIGHT . . . SEVEN . . . SIX . . . FIVE . . . OUR . . . THREE . . . TWO . . .

ONE, GUNTHER.

ONE, EH?

JANUARY 1, 2000

And so I am born.

I, Gabriel White, have come to stay.

Now that the terrible hole in my head has begun to

heal, I can get down to business. I wish the doctors would release me. My wound troubles them far less than their fear that I might still be a pathetic psychoneurotic. I am not. Gunther Black is dead.

Oh, to have seen Izzard's expression when Proletaria detonated its atomic bomb! But, alas, self-awareness did not reach me until after the shock wave had fissured Black's skull, and by then Izzard sat huddled in the corner, his face buried in his arms. A most spectacular advent, mine. The blast tore a piece of Black's brow away. It flew across the office like a pebble from a slingshot. Some brain dribbled out. Nothing crucial, the doctors tell me. French lessons, they think.

I am doing fine. The explosion has welded my fractured self whole. I am in command. Jeremy Green, Thomas Brown, Angela Lavender, Harry Silver . . . all five million of them know me and love me.

Happy New Year, everyone.

I must get to work. My people need direction and discipline—and occasionally a bit of torment. I'm going to start with Bernie Gold and his family.

Are you there, Bernie Gold? This is Gabriel White. I am the Lord thy God, who brought you out of the house of bondage. First of all, you will have no gods except me . . .

Are you getting this, Bernie? Do you hear me?

Yes?

Good.

Arms and the Woman

❖

"WHAT did you do in the war, Mommy?"

The last long shadow has slipped from the sundial's face, melting into the hot Egyptian night. My children should be asleep. Instead they're bouncing on their straw pallets, stalling for time.

"It's late," I reply. "Nine o'clock already."

"Please," the twins implore me in a single voice.

"You have school tomorrow."

"You haven't told us a story all week," insists Damon, the whiner.

"The war is such a *great* story," explains Daphne, the wheedler.

"Kaptah's mother tells *him* a story every night," whines Damon.

"Tell us about the war," wheedles Daphne, "and we'll clean the whole cottage tomorrow, top to bottom."

I realize I'm going to give in—not because I enjoy spoiling my children (though I do) or because the story itself will consume less time than further negotiations (though it will) but because I actually want the twins to hear this particular tale. It has a point. I've told it before, of course, a dozen times perhaps, but I'm still not sure they get it.

I snatch up the egg timer and invert it on the nightstand, the tiny grains of sand spilling into the lower chamber like seeds from a farmer's palm. "Be ready for bed in three minutes," I warn my children, "or no story."

They scurry off, frantically brushing their teeth and slipping on their flaxen nightshirts. Silently I glide about the cottage, dousing the lamps and curtaining the moon, until only one candle lights the twins' room, like the campfire of some small, pathetic army, an army of mice or scarab beetles.

"So you want to know what I did in the war," I intone, singsong, as my children climb into their beds.

"Oh, yes," says Damon, pulling up his fleecy coverlet.

"You bet," says Daphne, fluffing her goose-feather pillow.

"Once upon a time," I begin, "I lived as both princess and prisoner in the great city of Troy." Even in this feeble light, I'm struck by how handsome Damon is, how beautiful Daphne. "Every evening, I would sit in my boudoir, looking into my polished bronze mirror . . ."

Helen of Troy, princess and prisoner, sits in her boudoir, looking into her polished bronze mirror and scanning her world-class face for symptoms of age—for wrinkles, wattles, pouches, crow's-feet, and the crenelated corpses of hairs. She feels like crying, and not just because these past ten years in Ilium are starting to show. She's sick of the whole sordid arrangement, sick of being cooped up in this overheated acropolis like a pet cockatoo. Whispers haunt the citadel. The servants are gossiping, even her own handmaids. The whore of Hisarlik, they call her. The slut from Sparta. The Lakedaimon lay.

Then there's Paris. Sure, she's madly in love with him, sure, they have great sex, but can't they ever *talk?*

Sighing, Helen trolls her hairdo with her lean, exquisitely manicured fingers. A silver strand lies amid the folds like a predatory snake. Slowly she winds the offending filament around her index finger, then gives a sudden tug. "Ouch," she cries, more from despair than pain. There are times when Helen feels like tearing all her lovely tresses out, every last lock, not simply these graying threads. If I have to spend one more pointless day in Hisarlik, she tells herself, I'll go mad.

Every morning, she and Paris enact the same depressing ritual. She escorts him to the Skaian Gate, hands him his spear and his lunch bucket, and with a tepid kiss sends him off to work. Paris's job is killing people. At sundown he arrives home grubby with blood and redolent of funeral pyres, his spear wrapped in bits of drying viscera. There's a war going on out there; Paris won't tell her anything more. "Who are we fighting?" she asks each evening as they lie together in bed. "Don't you worry your pretty little head about it," he replies, slipping on a sheep-gut condom, the brand with the plumed and helmeted soldier on the box.

Until this year, Paris had wanted her to walk Troy's high walls each morning, waving encouragement to the troops, blowing them kisses as they marched off to battle. "Your face inspires them," he would insist. "An airy kiss from you is worth a thousand nights of passion with a nymph." But in recent months Paris's priorities have changed. As soon as they say good-bye, Helen is supposed to retire to the citadel, speaking with no other Hisarlikan, not even a brief coffee klatch with one of Paris's forty-nine sisters-in-law. She's expected to spend her whole day weaving rugs, carding flax, and being beautiful. It is not a life.

Can the gods help? Helen is skeptical, but anything is worth a try. Tomorrow, she resolves, she will go to the temple of Apollo and beg him to relieve her boredom, perhaps buttressing her appeal with an offering—a ram, a bull, whatever—though an offering strikes her as rather like a deal, and Helen is sick of deals. Her husband—pseudohusband, nonhusband—made a deal. She keeps thinking of the Apple of Discord, and what Aphrodite might have done with it after bribing Paris. Did she drop it in her fruit bowl . . . put it on her mantel . . . impale it on her crown? Why did Aphrodite take the damn thing seriously? Why did any of them take it seriously? Hi, I'm the fairest goddess in the universe— see, it says so right here on my apple.

Damn—another gray hair, another weed in the garden of her pulchritude. She reaches toward the villain—and stops. Why bother? These hairs are like the Hydra's heads, endless, cancerous, and besides, it's high time Paris realized there's a mind under that coiffure.

Whereupon Paris comes in, sweating and snorting. His helmet is awry; his spear is gory; his greaves are sticky with other men's flesh.

"Hard day, dear?"

"Don't ask." Her nonhusband unfastens his breastplate. "Pour us some wine. Looking in the speculum, were you? Good."

Helen sets the mirror down, uncorks the bottle, and fills two bejeweled goblets with Château Samothrace.

"Today I heard about some techniques you might try," says Paris. "Ways for a woman to retain her beauty."

"You mean—you *talk* on the battlefield?"

"During the lulls."

"I wish you'd talk to *me*."

"Wax," says Paris, lifting the goblet to his lips. "Wax is the thing." His heavy jowls undulate as he drinks. Their affair, Helen will admit, still gives her a kick. In the past ten years, her lover has moved beyond the surpassing prettiness of an Adonis into something equally appealing, an authoritative, no-frills masculinity suggestive of an aging matinee idol. "Take some melted wax and work it into the lines in your brow—presto, they're gone."

"I *like* my lines," Helen insists with a quick but audible snort.

"When mixed with ox blood, the dark silt from the River Minyeios is indelible, they say. You can dye your silver hairs back to auburn. A Grecian formula." Paris sips his wine. "As for these redundant ounces on your thighs, well, dear, we both know there's no cure like exercise."

"Look who's talking," Helen snaps. "*Your* skin is no bowl of cream. *Your* head is no garden of sargasso. As for your stomach, it's a safe bet that Paris of Troy can walk through the rain without getting his belt buckle wet."

The prince finishes his wine and sighs. "Where's the girl I married? You used to care about your looks."

"The girl you married," Helen replies pointedly, "is not your wife."

"Well, yes, of course not. Technically, you're still *his*."

"I want a wedding." Helen takes a gluttonous swallow of Samothrace and sets the goblet on the mirror. "You could go to my husband," she suggests. "You could present yourself to high-minded Menelaus and try to talk things out." Reflected in the mirror's wobbly face, the goblet grows weird, twisted, as if seen through a drunkard's eyes. "Hey, listen, I'll bet he's found another maid by now—he's something of a catch, after all. So maybe you actually did him a favor. Maybe he isn't even mad."

"He's mad," Paris insists. "The man is angry."

"How do you know?"

"I know."

Heedless of her royal station, Helen consumes her wine with the crude insouciance of a galley slave. "I want a baby," she says.

"What?"

"You know, a baby. *Baby:* a highly young person. My goal, dear Paris, is to be pregnant."

"Fatherhood is for losers." Paris chucks his spear onto the bed. Striking the mattress, the oaken shaft disappears into the soft down. "Go easy on the *vino,* love. Alcohol is awfully fattening."

"Don't you understand? I'm losing my mind. A pregnancy would give me a sense of purpose."

"Any idiot can sire a child. It takes a hero to defend a citadel."

"Have you found someone else, Paris? Is that it? Someone younger and thinner?"

"Don't be foolish. Throughout the whole of time, in days gone by and eras yet to come, no man will love a woman as much as Paris loves Helen."

"I'll bet the plains of Ilium are crawling with camp followers. They must swoon over you."

"Don't you worry your pretty little head about it," says Paris, unwrapping a plumed-soldier condom.

If he ever says that to me again, Helen vows as they tumble drunkenly into bed, I'll scream so loud the walls of Troy will fall.

———

The slaughter is not going well, and Paris is depressed. By his best reckoning, he's dispatched only fifteen Achaians to the house of Hades this morning: strong-greaved Machaon, iron-muscled Euchenor, ax-wielding Deichos, a dozen more—fifteen noble warriors sent to the dark depths, fifteen breathless bodies left to nourish the dogs and ravens. It is not enough.

All along the front, Priam's army is giving ground without a fight. Their morale is low, their *esprit* spent. They haven't seen Helen in a year, and they don't much feel like fighting anymore.

With a deep Aeolian sigh, the prince seats himself atop his pile of confiscated armor and begins his lunch break.

Does he have a choice? Must he continue keeping her in the shadows? Yes, by Poseidon's trident—yes. Exhibiting Helen as she looks now would just make matters worse. Once upon a time, her face launched a thousand ships. Today it couldn't get a Theban fishing schooner out of dry dock. Let the troops catch only a glimpse of her wrinkles, let them but glance at her aging hair, and they'll start deserting like rats leaving a foundering trireme.

He's polishing off a peach—since delivering his famous verdict and awarding Aphrodite her prize, Paris no longer cares for apples—when two of the finest horses in Hisarlik, Aithon and Xanthos, gallop up pulling his brother's war chariot. He expects to see Hector holding the reins, but no: the driver, he notes with a pang of surprise, is Helen.

"Helen? What are *you* doing here?"

Brandishing a cowhide whip, his lover jumps down. "You won't tell me what this war is about," she gasps, panting inside her armor, "so I'm investigating on my own. I just came from the swift-flowing Menderes, where your enemies are preparing to launch a cavalry charge against the camp of Epistrophos."

"Go back to the citadel, Helen. Go back to Pergamos."

"Paris, this army you're battling—they're *Greeks*. Idomeneus, Diomedes, Sthenelos, Euryalos, Odysseus— I *know* these men. Know them? By Pan's flute, I've *dated* half of them. You'll never guess who's about to lead that cavalry charge."

Paris takes a stab. "Agamemnon?"

"Agamemnon!" Sweat leaks from beneath Helen's helmet like blood from a scalp wound. "My own brother-in-law! Next you'll be telling me Menelaus himself has taken the field against Troy!"

Paris coughs and says, "Menelaus himself has taken the field against Troy."

"He's here?" wails Helen, thumping her breastplate. "My husband is *here?*"

"Correct."

"What's going on, Paris? For what purpose have the men of horse-pasturing Argos come all the way to Ilium?"

The prince bounces his peach pit off Helen's breastplate. Angrily he fishes for epithets. Mule-minded Helen, he calls her beneath his breath. Leather-skinned Lake-daimon. He feels beaten and bettered, trapped and teth-ered. "Very well, sweetheart, very well . . ." Helen of the iron will, the hard ass, the bronze bottom. "They've come for *you*, love."

"What?"

"For you."

"Me? What are you talking about?"

"They want to steal you back." As Paris speaks, Helen's waning beauty seems to drop another notch. Her face darkens with an unfathomable mix of anger, hurt, and confusion. "They're pledged to it. King Tyndareus made your suitors swear they'd be loyal to whomever you selected as husband."

"*Me?*" Helen leaps into the chariot. "You're fighting an entire, stupid, disgusting war for *me?*"

"Well, not for you per se. For honor, for glory, for arete. Now hurry off to Pergamos—that's an order."

"I'm hurrying off, dear"—she raises her whip—"but not to Pergamos. On, Aithon!" She snaps the lash. "On, Xanthos!"

"Then where?"

Instead of answering, Paris's lover speeds away, leav-ing him to devour her dust.

Dizzy with outrage, trembling with remorse, Helen charges across the plains of Ilium. On all sides, an aston-ishing drama unfolds, a spectacle of shattered senses and violated flesh: soldiers with eyes gouged out, tongues cut

loose, limbs hacked off, bellies ripped open; soldiers, as
it were, giving birth to their own bowels—all because of
her. She weeps openly, profusely, the large gemlike tears
running down her wrinkled cheeks and striking her
breastplate. The agonies of Prometheus are a picnic compared to the weight of her guilt, the Pillars of Herakles
are feathers when balanced against the crushing tonnage
of her conscience.

Honor, glory, arete: I'm missing something, Helen realizes as she surveys the carnage. The essence eludes me.

She reaches the thick and stinking Lisgar Marsh and
reins up before a foot soldier sitting in the mud, a young
Myrmidon with what she assumes are a particularly honorable spear hole in his breastplate and a singularly glorious lack of a right hand.

"Can you tell me where I might find your king?" she
asks.

"By Hera's eyes, you're easy to look at," gasps the
soldier as, arete in full bloom, he binds his bleeding
stump with linen.

"I need to find Menelaus."

"Try the harbor," he says, gesturing with his wound.
The bandaged stump drips like a leaky faucet. "His ship
is the *Arkadia*."

Helen thanks the soldier and aims her horses toward
the wine-dark sea.

"Are you Helen's mother, by any chance?" he calls
as she races off. "What a face you've got!"

Twenty minutes later, reeling with thirst and smelling

of horse sweat, Helen pulls within view of the crashing waves. In the harbor beyond, a thousand strong-hulled ships lie at anchor, their masts jutting into the sky like a forest of denuded trees. All along the beach, Helen's countrymen are raising a stout wooden wall, evidently fearful that, if the line is ever pushed back this far, the Trojans will not hesitate to burn the fleet. The briny air rings with the Achaians' axes—with the thud and crunch of acacias being felled, palisades being whittled, stockade posts sharpened, breastworks shaped, a cacophony muffling the flutter of the sails and the growl of the surf.

Helen starts along the wharf, soon spotting the *Arkadia*, a stout penteconter with half a hundred oars bristling from her sides like quills on a hedgehog. No sooner has she crossed the gangplank than she comes upon her husband, older now, striated by wrinkles, but still unquestionably he. Plumed like a peacock, Menelaus stands atop the forecastle, speaking with a burly construction brigade, tutoring them in the proper placement of the impalement stakes. A handsome man, she decides, much like the warrior on the condom boxes. She can see why she picked him over Sthenelos, Euryalos, and her other beaus.

As the workers set off to plant their spiky groves, Helen saunters up behind Menelaus and taps his shoulder.

"Hi," she says.

He was always a wan fellow, but now his face loses whatever small quantity of blood it once possessed.

"Helen?" he says, gasping and blinking like a man who's just been doused with a bucket of slop. "Is that *you?*"

"Right."

"You've, er . . . aged."

"You too, sweetheart."

He pulls off his plumed helmet, stomps his foot on the forecastle, and says, angrily, "You ran out on me."

"Yes. Quite so."

"Trollop."

"Perhaps." Helen adjusts her greaves. "I could claim I was bewitched by laughter-loving Aphrodite, but that would be a lie. The fact is, Paris knocked me silly. I'm crazy about him. Sorry." She runs her desiccated tongue along her parched lips. "Have you anything to drink?"

Dipping a hollow gourd into his private cistern, Menelaus offers her a pint of fresh water. "So what brings you here?"

Helen receives the ladle. Setting her boots wide apart, she steadies herself against the roll of the incoming tide and takes a greedy gulp. At last she says, "I wish to give myself up."

"What?"

"I want to go home with you."

"You mean—you think our marriage deserves another chance?"

"No, I think all those infantrymen out there deserve to live. If this war is really being fought to retrieve me, then consider the job done." Tossing the ladle aside, Helen holds out her hands, palms turned upward as if she's testing for raindrops. "I'm yours, hubby. Manacle my wrists, chain my feet together, throw me in the brig."

Against all odds, defying all *logos,* Menelaus's face loses more blood. "I don't think that's a very good idea," he says.

"Huh? What do you mean?"

"This siege, Helen—there's more to it than you suppose."

"Don't jerk me around, lord of all Lakedaimon, asshole. It's time to call it quits."

The Spartan king stares straight at her chest, a habit she's always found annoying. "Put on a bit of weight, eh, darling?"

"Don't change the subject." She lunges toward Menelaus's scabbard as if to goose him, but instead draws out his sword. "I'm deadly serious: if Helen of Troy is not permitted to live with herself"—she pantomimes the act of suicide—"then she will die with herself."

"Tell you what," says her husband, taking his weapon back. "Tomorrow morning, first thing, I'll go to my brother and suggest he arrange a truce with your father-in-law."

"He's not my father-in-law. There was never a wedding."

"Whatever. The point is, your offer has merit, but it must be discussed. We shall all meet face-to-face, Trojans and Achaians, and talk it out. As for now, you'd best return to your lover."

"I'm warning you—I shall abide no more blood on my hands, none but my own."

"Of course, dear. Now please go back to the citadel."

At least he listened, Helen muses as she crosses the weatherworn deck of the *Arkadia*. At least he didn't tell me not to worry my pretty little head about it.

"Here comes the dull part," says whiny-tongued Damon.

"The scene with all the talking," adds smart-mouthed Daphne.

"Can you cut it a bit?" my son asks.

"Hush," I say, smoothing out Damon's coverlet. "No interruptions," I insist. I slip Daphne's papyrus doll under her arm. "When you have your own children, you can edit the tale however you wish. As for now, listen carefully. You might learn something."

By the burbling, tumbling waters of the River Simois, beneath the glowing orange avatar of the moon goddess Artemis, ten aristocrats are gathered around an oaken table in the purple tent of Ilium's high command, all of them bursting with opinions on how best to deal with this Helen situation, this peace problem, this Trojan hostage crisis. White as a crane, a truce banner flaps above the heads of the two kings, Priam from the high city, Agamemnon from the long ships. Each side has sent its best and/or brightest. For the Trojans: brainy Panthoös, mighty Paris, invincible Hector, and Hiketaon the scion of Ares. For the Achaian cause: Ajax the berserker,

Nestor the mentor, Menelaus the cuckold, and wily, smiling Odysseus. Of all those invited, only quarrelsome Achilles, sulking in his tent, has declined to appear.

Panthoös rises, rubs his foam-white beard, and sets his scepter on the table. "Royal captains, gifted seers," the old Trojan begins, "I believe you will concur when I say that, since this siege was laid, we have not faced a challenge of such magnitude. Make no mistake: Helen means to take our war away from us, and she means to do so immediately."

Gusts of dismay waft through the tent like a wind from the underworld.

"We can't quit now," groans Hector, wincing fiercely.

"We're just getting up to speed," wails Hiketaon, grimacing greatly.

Agamemnon steps down from his throne, carrying his scepter like a spear. "I have a question for Prince Paris," he says. "What does your mistress's willingness to return to Argos say about the present state of your relationship?"

Paris strokes his jowls and replies, "As you might surmise, noble King, my feelings for Helen are predicated on requitement."

"So you won't keep her in Pergamos by force?"

"If she doesn't want me, then I don't want her."

At which point slug-witted Ajax raises his hand. "Er, excuse me. I'm a bit confused. If Helen is ours for the asking, then why must we continue the war?"

A sirocco of astonishment arises among the heroes.

"Why?" gasps Panthoös. "*Why?* Because this is *Troy*, that's why. Because we're kicking off Western Civilization here, that's why. The longer we can keep this affair going—the longer we can sustain such an ambiguous enterprise—the more valuable and significant it becomes."

Slow-synapsed Ajax says, "Huh?"

Nestor has but to clear his throat and every eye is upon him. "What our adversary is saying—may I interpret, wise Panthoös?" He turns to his Trojan counterpart, bows deferentially, and, receiving a nod of assent, speaks to Ajax. "Panthoös means that, if this particular pretext for war—restoring a woman to her rightful owner—can be made to seem reasonable, then *any* pretext for war can be made to seem reasonable." The mentor shifts his fevered stare from Ajax to the entire assembly. "By rising to this rare and precious occasion, we shall open the way for wars of religion, wars of manifest destiny—any equivocal cause you care to name." Once again his gaze alights on Ajax. "Understand, sir? This is the war to inaugurate war itself. This is the war to make the world safe for war!"

Ajax frowns so vigorously his visor falls down. "All I know is, we came for Helen, and we got her. Mission accomplished." Turning to Agamemnon, the berserker lifts the visor from his eyes. "So if it's all the same to you, Majesty, I'd like to go home before I get killed."

"O, Ajax, Ajax, Ajax," moans Hector, pulling an arrow from his quiver and using it to scratch his back.

"Where is your aesthetic sense? Have you no apprecia-
tion of war for war's sake? The plains of Ilium are roiling
with glory, sir. You could cut the arete with a knife.
Never have there been such valiant eviscerations, such
venerable dismemberments, such—"

"I don't get it," says the berserker. "I just don't
get it."

Whereupon Menelaus slams his wine goblet on the
table with a resounding thunk. "We are not gathered in
Priam's tent so that Ajax might learn politics," he says
impatiently. "We are gathered so that we might best dispose of my wife."

"True, true," says Hector.

"So what are we going to do, gentlemen?" asks
Menelaus. "Lock her up?"

"Good idea," says Hiketaon.

"Well, yes," says Agamemnon, slumping back onto
his throne. "Except that, when the war finally ends, my
troops will demand to see her. Might they not wonder
why so much suffering and sacrifice was spent on a goddess gone to seed?" He turns to Paris and says, "Prince,
you should not have let this happen."

"Let *what* happen?" asks Paris.

"I heard she has wrinkles," says Agamemnon.

"I heard she got fat," says Nestor.

"What have you been feeding her?" asks Menelaus.
"Bonbons?"

"She's a *person*," protests Paris. "She's not a marble
statue. You can hardly blame *me* . . ."

At which juncture King Priam raises his scepter and, as if to wound Gaea herself, rams it into the dirt.

"Noble lords, I hate to say this, but the threat is more immediate than you might suppose. In the early years of the siege, the sight of fair Helen walking the ramparts did wonders for my army's morale. Now that she's no longer fit for public display, well . . ."

"Yes?" says Agamemnon, steeling himself for the worst.

"Well, I simply don't know how much longer Troy can hold up its end of the war. If things don't improve, we may have to capitulate by next winter."

Gasps of horror blow across the table, rattling the tent flaps and ruffling the aristocrats' capes.

But now, for the first time, clever, canny Odysseus addresses the council, and the winds of discontent grow still. "Our course is obvious," he says. "Our destiny is clear," he asserts. "We must put Helen—the old Helen, the pristine Helen—back on the walls."

"The pristine Helen?" says Hiketaon. "Are you not talking fantasy, resourceful Odysseus? Are you not singing a myth?"

The lord of all Ithaca strolls the length of Priam's tent, plucking at his beard. "It will require some wisdom from Pallas Athena, some technology from Hephaestus, but I believe the project is possible."

"Excuse me," says Paris. "*What* project is possible?"

"Refurbishing your little harlot," says Odysseus. "Making the dear, sweet strumpet shine like new."

Back and forth, to and fro, Helen moves through her boudoir, wearing a ragged path of angst into the carpet. An hour passes. Then two. Why are they taking so long?

What most gnaws at her, the thought that feasts on her entrails, is the possibility that, should the council not accept her surrender, she will have to raise the stakes. And how might she accomplish the deed? By what means might she book passage on Charon's one-way ferry? Something from her lover's arsenal, most likely—a sword, spear, dagger, or death-dripping arrow. O, please, my lord Apollo, she prays to the city's prime protector, don't let it come to that.

At sunset Paris enters the room, his pace leaden, his jowls dragging his mouth into a grimace. For the first time ever, Helen observes tears in her lover's eyes.

"It is finished," he moans, doffing his plumed helmet. "Peace has come. At dawn you must go to the long ships. Menelaus will bear you back to Sparta, where you will once again live as mother to his children, friend to his concubines, and emissary to his bed."

Relief pours out of Helen in a deep, orgasmic rush, but the pleasure is short-lived. She loves this man, flaws and all, flab and the rest. "I shall miss you, dearest Paris," she tells him. "Your bold abduction of me remains the peak experience of my life."

"I agreed to the treaty only because Menelaus believes you might otherwise kill yourself. You're a surprising woman, Helen. Sometimes I think I hardly know you."

"Hush, my darling," she says, gently placing her palm across his mouth. "No more words."

Slowly they unclothe each other, methodically unlocking the doors to bliss, the straps and sashes, the snaps and catches, and thus begins their final, epic night together.

"I'm sorry I've been so judgmental," says Paris.

"I accept your apology."

"You are so beautiful. So impossibly beautiful . . ."

As dawn's rosy fingers stretch across the Trojan sky, Hector's faithful driver, Eniopeus the son of horse-loving Thebaios, steers his sturdy war chariot along the banks of the Menderes, bearing Helen to the Achaian stronghold. They reach the *Arkadia* just as the sun is cresting, so their arrival in the harbor becomes a flaming parade, a show of sparks and gold, as if they ride upon the burning wheels of Hyperion himself.

Helen starts along the dock, moving past the platoons of squawking gulls adrift on the early morning breeze. Menelaus comes forward to greet her, accompanied by a man for whom Helen has always harbored a vague dislike—broad-chested, black-bearded Teukros, illegitimate son of Telemon.

"The tide is ripe," says her husband. "You and Teukros must board forthwith. You will find him a lively traveling companion. He knows a hundred fables and plays the harp."

"Can't *you* take me home?"

Menelaus squeezes his wife's hand and, raising it to his lips, plants a gentle kiss. "I must see to the loading of my ships," he explains, "the disposition of my battalions—a full week's job, I'd guess."

"Surely you can leave that to Agamemnon."

"Give me seven days, Helen. In seven days I'll be home, and we can begin picking up the pieces."

"We're losing the tide," says Teukros, anxiously intertwining his fingers.

Do I trust my husband? wonders Helen as she strides up the *Arkadia*'s gangplank. Does he really mean to lift the siege?

All during their slow voyage out of the harbor, Helen is haunted. Nebulous fears, nagging doubts, and odd presentiments swarm through her brain like Harpies. She beseeches her beloved Apollo to speak with her, calm her, assure her all is well, but the only sounds reaching her ears are the creaking of the oars and the windy, watery voice of the Hellespont.

By the time the *Arkadia* finds the open sea, Helen has resolved to jump overboard and swim back to Troy.

"And then Teukros tried to kill you," says Daphne.

"He came at you with his sword," adds Damon.

This is the twins' favorite part, the moment of grue and gore. Eyes flashing, voice climbing to a melodramatic pitch, I tell them how, before I could put my escape plan into action, Teukros began chasing me around the *Arkadia*, slashing his two-faced blade. I tell them how I got the upper hand, tripping the bastard as he was about to run me through.

"You stabbed him with his own sword, didn't you, Mommy?" asks Damon.

"I had no choice."

"And then his guts spilled, huh?" asks Daphne.

"Agamemnon had ordered Teukros to kill me," I explain. "I was ruining everything."

"They spilled out all over the deck, right?" asks Damon.

"Yes, dear, they certainly did. I'm quite convinced Paris wasn't part of the plot, or Menelaus either. Your mother falls for fools, not maniacs."

"What color were they?" asks Damon.

"Color?"

"His guts."

"Red, mostly, with daubs of purple and black."

"Neat."

I tell the twins of my long, arduous swim through the strait.

I tell them how I crossed Ilium's war-torn fields, dodging arrows and eluding patrols.

I tell how I waited by the Skaian Gate until a farmer arrived with a cartload of provender for the besieged city . . . how I sneaked inside the walls, secluded amid stalks of wheat . . . how I went to Pergamos, hid myself in the temple of Apollo, and breathlessly waited for dawn.

Dawn comes up, binding the eastern clouds in crimson girdles. Helen leaves the citadel, tiptoes to the wall, and mounts the hundred granite steps to the battlements. She is unsure of her next move. She has some vague hope of addressing the infantrymen as they assemble at the gate. Her arguments have failed to impress the generals, but perhaps she can touch the heart of the common foot soldier.

It is at this ambiguous point in her fortunes that Helen runs into herself.

She blinks—once, twice. She swallows a sphere of air. Yes, it is she, herself, marching along the parapets. Herself? No, not exactly: an idealized rendition, the Helen of ten years ago, svelte and smooth.

As the troops march through the portal and head toward the plain, the strange incarnation calls down to them.

"Onward, men!" it shouts, raising a creamy white arm. "Fight for me!" Its movements are deliberate and jerky, as if sunbaked Troy has been magically transplanted to some frigid clime. "I'm worth it!"

The soldiers turn, look up. "We'll fight for you, Helen!" a bowman calls toward the parapet.

"We love you!" a sword-wielder shouts.

Awkwardly, the incarnation waves. Creakily, it

blows an arid kiss. "Onward, men! Fight for me! I'm worth it!"

"You're beautiful, Helen!" a spear-thrower cries.

Helen strides up to her doppelgänger and, seizing the left shoulder, pivots the creature toward her.

"Onward, men!" it tells Helen. "Fight for me! I'm worth it!"

"You're beautiful," the spear-thrower continues, "and so is your mother!"

The eyes, Helen is not surprised to discover, are glass. The limbs are fashioned from wood, the head from marble, the teeth from ivory, the lips from wax, the tresses from the fleece of a darkling ram. Helen does not know for certain what forces power this creature, what magic moves its tongue, but she surmises that the genius of Athena is at work here, the witchery of ox-orbed Hera. Chop the creature open, she senses, and out will pour a thousand cogs and pistons from Hephaestus's fiery workshop.

Helen wastes no time. She hugs the creature, lifts it off its feet. Heavy, but not so heavy as to dampen her resolve.

"Onward, men!" it screams as Helen throws it over her shoulder. "Fight for me! I'm worth it!"

And so it comes to pass that, on a hot, sweaty Asia Minor morning, fair Helen turns the tables on history, gleefully abducting herself from the lofty stone city of Troy.

Paris is pulling a poisoned arrow from his quiver, intent on shooting a dollop of hemlock into the breast of an Achaian captain, when his brother's chariot charges past.

Paris nocks the arrow. He glances at the chariot.

He aims.

Glances again.

Fires. Misses.

Helen.

Helen? *Helen,* by Apollo's lyre, his Helen—no, two Helens, the true and the false, side by side, the true guiding the horses into the thick of the fight, her wooden twin staring dreamily into space. Paris can't decide which woman he is more astonished to see.

"Soldiers of Troy!" cries the fleshy Helen. "Heroes of Argos! Behold how your leaders seek to dupe you! You are fighting for a fraud, a swindle, a thing of gears and glass!"

A stillness envelops the battlefield. The men are stunned, not so much by the ravings of the charioteer as by the face of her companion, so pure and perfect despite the leather thong sealing her jaw shut. It is a face to sheathe a thousand swords—lower a thousand spears—unnock a thousand arrows.

Which is exactly what now happens. A thousand swords: sheathed. A thousand spears: lowered. A thousand arrows: unnocked.

The soldiers crowd around the chariot, pawing at the ersatz Helen. They touch the wooden arms, caress the marble brow, stroke the ivory teeth, pat the waxen lips, squeeze the woolly hair, rub the glass eyes.

"See what I mean?" cries the true Helen. "Your kings are diddling you . . ."

Paris can't help it: he's proud of her, by Hermes's wings. He's puffing up with admiration. This woman has nerve—she has arete and chutzpah.

This woman, Paris realizes as a fat, warm tear of nostalgia rolls down his cheek, is going to the end the war.

"The end," I say.

"And then what happened?" Damon asks.

"Nothing. *Finis.* Go to sleep."

"You can't fool us," says Daphne. "All *sorts* of things happened after that. You went to live on the island of Lesbos."

"Not immediately," I note. "I wandered the world for seven years, having many fine and fabulous adventures. Good night."

"And then you went to Lesbos," Daphne insists.

"And then *we* came into the world," Damon asserts.

"True," I say. The twins are always interested in hearing how they came into the world. They never tire of the tale.

"The women of Lesbos import over a thousand liters of frozen semen annually," Damon explains to Daphne.

"From Thrace," Daphne explains to Damon.

"In exchange for olives."

"A thriving trade."

"Right, honey," I say. "Bedtime."

"And so you got pregnant," says Daphne.

"And had us," says Damon.

"And brought us to Egypt." Daphne tugs at my sleeve as if operating a bell rope. "I came out first, didn't I?" she says. "I'm the *oldest*."

"Yes, dear."

"Is that why I'm smarter than Damon?"

"You're both equally smart. I'm going to blow out the candle now."

Daphne hugs her papyrus doll and says, "Did you really end the war?"

"The treaty was signed the day after I fled Troy. Of course, peace didn't restore the dead, but at least Troy was never sacked and burned. Now go to sleep—both of you."

Damon says, "Not before we've . . ."

"What?"

"You know."

"All right," I say. "One quick peek, and then you're off to the land of Morpheus."

I saunter over to the closet and, drawing back the linen curtain, reveal my stalwart twin standing upright amid the children's robes. She smiles through the gloom. She's a tireless smiler, this woman.

"Hi, Aunt Helen!" says Damon as I throw the bronze toggle protruding from the nape of my sister's neck.

She waves to my children and says, "Onward, men! Fight for me!"

"You bet, Aunt Helen!" says Daphne.

"I'm worth it!" says my sister.

"You sure are!" says Damon.

"Onward, men! Fight for me! I'm worth it!"

I switch her off and close the curtain. Tucking in the twins, I give each a big soupy kiss on the cheek. "Love you, Daphne. Love you, Damon."

I start to douse the candle—stop. As long as it's on my mind, I should get the chore done. Returning to the closet, I push the curtain aside, lift the penknife from my robe, and pry back the blade. And then, as the Egyptian night grows moist and thick, I carefully etch yet another wrinkle across my sister's brow, right beneath her salt-and-pepper bangs.

It's important, after all, to keep up appearances.

Publication Acknowledgments

The stories in this collection first appeared in the following publications:

"Bible Stories for Adults, No. 17: The Deluge"—*Full Spectrum* (New York: Bantam Books, 1988)

"Daughter Earth"—*Full Spectrum 3* (New York: Bantam Books, 1991)

"Known But to God and Wilbur Hines"—*There Won't Be War* (New York: Tor, 1991)

"Bible Stories for Adults, No. 20: The Tower"—*Swatting at the Cosmos* (Eugene, OR: Pulphouse Publishing, 1990). Revised version published in *The Magazine of Fantasy and Science Fiction* (June 1994).

"Spelling God with the Wrong Blocks"—*The Magazine of Fantasy and Science Fiction* (May 1987)

"The Assemblage of Kristin"—*Isaac Asimov's Science Fiction Magazine* (June 1984)

"Bible Stories for Adults, No. 31: The Covenant"—*Aboriginal Science Fiction* (November-December 1989)

"Abe Lincoln in McDonald's"—*The Magazine of Fantasy and Science Fiction* (May 1989)

"The Confessions of Ebenezer Scrooge"—*Spirits of Christmas* (New York: Wynwood Press, 1989)

"Bible Stories for Adults, No. 46: The Soap Opera"—*God: An Anthology of Fiction* (London: Serpent's Tail, 1992). Revised version published in *Science Fiction Age* (January 1994).

"Diary of a Mad Deity"—*Synergy Number 2* (San Diego: Harcourt Brace Jovanovich, 1988)

"Arms and the Woman"—*Amazing Stories* (July 1991)